Theodore F. Lee brings to the writing world a wonderful vision, influenced by countless occupations. His writing material has been chiseled from a colorful palette of life experiences, which took this author from the hard labor of fishing rooms to the hallowed halls of university classrooms. Emerging from those many experiences, he reconstructs a literary picture that excites the imagination with the turn of each page and the conclusion of every chapter. Even though Theodore has achieved multiple university degrees, including a master's degree in education, he believes that the true path to a fulfilled life comes from the space between the pages of life.

To my grandson Brooks – may he always see the world
with clear eyes and an open heart.

To my readers – may they always see the world with the
eyes of clarity and the heart of a child.

Theodore F. Lee

MURDER ON WOLF OWL BANK

AUSTIN MACAULEY PUBLISHERS™
LONDON • CAMBRIDGE • NEW YORK • SHARJAH

Ordering Information
Quantity sales: Special discounts are available on quantity purchases by corporations, associations, and others. For details, contact the publisher at the address below.

Publisher's Cataloging-in-Publication data
Lee, Theodore F.
Murder on Wolf Owl Bank

ISBN 9798889102267 (Paperback)
ISBN 9798891553378 (ePub e-book)

Library of Congress Control Number: 2024901477

www.austinmacauley.com/us

First Published 2024
Austin Macauley Publishers LLC
40 Wall Street, 33rd Floor, Suite 3302
New York, NY 10005
USA

mail-usa@austinmacauley.com
+1 (646) 5125767

Table of Contents

Chapter 1
Foggy Suspicions

It was spring in Newfoundland, when the men and women of Slate Harbour woke every morning to find fog as far as the eye could see. In a place where the cold Labrador current from the north churned with the warm Gulf stream from the south, to produce the foggiest place on earth, it was normal to see nothing as they prepared for another day of fishing. Just like the spring flowers that clung to the shale cliffs overlooking their foggy little fishing community, it was part of everyday life, and they accepted it with open arms.

Slate Harbour was precariously perched on the hilly rocks overlooking the deep frigid waters of Newfoundland. It was a place steeped in the traditional ways of a fishery that existed for hundreds of years. From a time when the best of navigation could only offer up the stars in the sky to a time when global positioning satellites could place them anytime and anywhere, the uncertainty of the fishery didn't change with technology. The men and women of Slate Harbour simply remained side by side with an old cod fishery that went up and down with the whims of nature.

On an ordinary spring morning, Martha Morgan looked out from the window and, while filling the kettle, she said, "She's as thick as pea soup this morn'n, Michael." Her husband never replied; he just twisted in his old wooden chair, and shouted, "GET YER ARSE OUT OF BED, BOY!" He twisted back towards his wife of twenty years, and said, "I'm getting sick of dis bullshit…" Mrs. Morgan placed the large kettle on the stove and asked, "Are ya sure he's rob'n yer nets?"

"I know it's him… That louse-bound bastard never changed one little bit…" He placed his teacup on the table and finished, "Not since we were young lads, fish'n fer tom-cods off da wharf…"

She picked up his empty cup and reminded him, "But nobody has ever caught him red-handed yet!"

He stood up from the table with a warning, "Oh… I'll catch 'em… and when I do, I'll…"

Young Matthew stumbled into the white-walled kitchen, rubbing his eyes, "What's for breakfast, Mudder?"

Matthew's father grabbed his coat, opened the thick-painted door, and answered for his wife, "Too late for grub now… You'll eat when we gets back from fish'n."

Martha placed a raisin tea bun into Matthew's hand, gave him a half smile, and said, "Watch out for yer father; he's got Sam Black stuck in his craw again…" Matthew grinned at his mother and said, "Don't worry, Mudder, Fadder's all talk and no action…" He walked out into the chilly fog and headed for the stage-head down by the water's edge, where his father was turning over their John Deere engine. With a puff of black smoke from the engine stack and an exhale from his unfiltered camel cigarette, Michael Morgan growled, "LET ER GO, MATTY!"

The fog may have been heavy that morning, but the sea was as calm as oil. Normally, when the spring fog rolled in the bays and inlets, it meant smooth sailing waters. In the past, it also meant the arrival of numerous cod seeking the spring caplin. For years and years, the caplin spawning ritual came like clockwork. They arrived year after year with the spring fog and then spawned on the sandy beaches that dotted the rugged coastline. The hungry cod were usually close behind, licking every rock along the way until they finally caught up with the caplin in shoal waters. It was an age-old routine, where the dying caplin came to spawn every year on the beaches, and cod would feed on them until they were swollen to capacity. On that day, in the dense fog just outside of Slate Harbour, it was plain to see that the times had changed. It had become very evident for the foundering fishermen that the migratory cycle was certainly broken.

Michael Morgan hauled back on the throttle, and the Morgan's Pride came to a slow soak in the calm cold waters. From the cover of low-lying fog, the sister vessel of the Morgan's Pride appeared and slowly approached. Side by side and at close quarters, Michael Morgan quickly glanced down at the height of the waterline and then looked skyward in silent desperation. With only the smell of seaweed and saltwater in the air, his brother Gus declared, "They're as scarce as hen's teeth, Mic!"

"Yes b'y... And get'n scarcer, with that bloody scavenger around..."

Gus looked out into a blanket of fog, and replied, "Well, nobody knows for sure if he's rob'n da nets…"

"Oh… I know it's him… And when I catch that bastard, I'll…"

"BANG!" Gus slammed his gaff down hard upon the deck and said, "KNOCK IT OFF, BROTHER! You're go'na get yerself in trouble with that talk! That guy is crazy…"

"Not as crazy as me, if I catch him at my nets…"

Gus Morgan pushed the Morgan's Pride away with his gaff and shoved his diesel in forward gear. He had heard enough from his brother for one day. Gus Morgan wasn't worried about the possibility of a phantom net robber. He was worried about what his brother would do if he actually caught Sam Black in action. Gus white-knuckled the engine throttle and placed his brother in a wake of uncertainty as he headed home with a dry fish hole and a pounding headache.

The Morgan's Pride plowed on toward their cod nets that were positioned on the shoal of the fishing bank. In the past, that shoal had been the best location where full nets could be guaranteed. Even when fish were few and far between, that shoal always produced good fishing results. However, on that morning before they pulled their nets, Michael Morgan's confidence sunk like a heavy lead jigger after sighting something that wasn't right.

Off to the port, he caught a glimpse of Sam Black's green boat slipping under the cover of the heavy fog. Michael Morgan was convinced it was Sam Black, and Mathew knew it, by the look of his father's flushed face.

With white foam pouring from the sides of his mouth, he shouted, "THAT BLOODY BASTARD!"

"Forget him, Fadder! Let's just haul our nets and leave that boat be…"

"You don't understand Son… There's nut'n in these nets now… Nut'n."

Young Matthew latched onto the buoy and spun it around the hydraulic hauler, "Haul 'em in, Fadder."

Ten nets later and nothing to show, only a few scrawny tom cods and some smelly sculpins. It was another day of hauling nets and getting nothing but a load of desperation and despair. With the smell of sculpin juice in the air and the slow roll of their boat on the foggy water, young Matthew continued to pile the empty nets behind his father. As the time soaked by, he dove deeper into murky waters between his father and Sam Black.

"Why do you always think he's rob'n our nets?"

"'Cause he's da only prick who would do it."

"Maybe it's just because there's no fish at all?"

Matthew's father pointed towards the empty fish hold, "She's scarce, all right, but not that scarce…"

"As long as I can remember you never liked him…"

"No, Matty… I don't like da cut of his jib."

"But why, Fadder?"

His father looked out upon the horizon, and before he could answer his son, there was a loud bang from the hydraulic winch, followed by a hissing spray of hydraulic fluid. In the middle of coming clean with his son, their net hauler blew a main hose and began to blow fluid over everything in sight. The busted hydraulic hose rattled across the deck, hissing and spraying slippery fluid in every direction. Every spray from the slithering hose quickly increased the danger of injury upon the slippery deck.

Michael Morgan knew the spewing fluid from the flailing hose was not the only immediate problem. There was a stainless-steel connector on the end of the hydraulic hose, and with every swoop of the agitated hose, the danger of receiving a lethal blow from its steel end increased. Without hesitation, Michael Morgan danced with danger and headed directly for the head of the problem. Jumping over the slithering hose, he failed to keep his footing on the soaked deck. The stainless connecter sliced by the side of the fallen father, and before it struck out for the final blow, it fell to the feet of its beaten foe. In the midst of the slippery attack, young Matthew Morgan shut the engine down, and with that, he had cut off the oil supply to the renegade hose.

As the brightness battled to penetrate the thick Newfoundland fog, the glossy aftermath was clear to see. Dripping in oil and soaking in a sea of shame, Michael Morgan sat in deep reflection. He'd taken his chance with a hose worn to the quick, leaving them with a close-call injury and no hauler to retrieve the remaining nets. Young Matthew carefully stepped out from the wheelhouse and with encouragement, he said, "Come on, Fadder, we'll haul them by hand."

His father put up his arms in frustration and exclaimed, "We don't have money to keep this bloody boat afloat…"

"Let's not worry about that now, Fadder…"

Michael Morgan wiped his hands off in his oil-soaked jeans, grabbed onto the hanging net, and said, "Start haul'n, Son…"

Every slow-rising swell brought another bout of agony for father and son as they latched onto the net to keep it from relenting back into the sea. Heaving and hauling to gain inch for inch but finding a lost cause of no fish, the cramps grew tighter upon their faces. Finally, with his foot stamped between the net and the gunwale to hold the strain, Michael Morgan cried out:

"THAT BASTARD, SAM BLACK!"

Startled but composed, Matthew responded, "Maybe, it's just because there's no fish to be had, Fadder!"

"ARE YA BLIND, BOY?" His father released the net with his bleeding hands and continued, "Didn't you see his boat slip'n under da cover of fog?" Matthew put his head down and slowly replied, "I'm not sure if it was him and I don't know if he hauled our nets…"

Michael Morgan grabbed onto the net, and without syncing himself to the rising swell, he hauled, while mumbling under his breath, "Oh… I know it was him… And I'll get him for it…" Young Matthew looked at his father strangely and slowly asked, "What will you do, Fadder?" His father never answered. He continued to pull the nets by hand, and with every painful grasp, the stinging salt water seared Sam Black deep into the cracks of his mind.

It was late when the Morgan's Pride pulled alongside the wharf in Slate Harbour. The wharf was like their empty fish hold, dry and without any evidence of slippery cod. The fishermen had come and gone earlier, leaving no trace of how much fish they caught or who had caught it. Normally, the onlookers would be on the wharf watching each boat offload the catch, but with the Morgan's Pride behind time, the onlookers were late coming. Tom the bull was the first to perch on the wharf's edge and check out the Morgan's Pride empty fish hold. After a short scan, Tom the bull lit up his unfiltered cigarette and said, "She's not good today, hey Mic…"

Michael Morgan hitched a bowline on his boat and replied without looking, "She's not good any day, these days Tom…"

Tom the bull took a strong inhale that seemed to go right to his rubber boots, and after a time, he exhaled with a cloud of smoke. "Well… I remember a time when fish holds like yours would be filled to da brim every day…"

Young Matthew chimed in, "Maybe those days will come again… Hey, Fadder…"

Another cloud of smoke permeated the wharf, and with it, another fisherman perched alongside Tom the bull. With a quick assessment of the sad surroundings, Uncle Price began, "She's gone, b'y…" Tom the bull was quick to add, "And she wouldn't be come'n back anytime soon…"

From the shadow of the weighmaster's winch, a familiar voice shouted down toward the deck. "WHAT'S GONE!" A cloak of expected silence descended upon the wharf, as the familiar voice continued, "Why all the doom and gloom fellers?"

Sam Black stepped out from the shadow and wedged himself between Tom the bull and Uncle Price. They responded quickly by giving him a wide berth with a silent stare.

Pretending to look down into the Morgan's Pride fish hold, Sam Black slyly pointed out the obvious, "Ah... I see... No fish again, Morgan!" Without any response, Black continued, "Well, she's not all, doom and gloom, b'y!" Still with no comments, he went on, "Sure, I caught meself a full load of cod today!" Knowing he couldn't crack a comment from anyone, he tried a different approach to, once again, rub salt into sore wounds, "Are ya fish'n with no hooks, Morgan?" There was silence. "Are yer nets upside down then?"

There was no need for any support from Tom the bull or Uncle Price; Sam Black put on his own show and became his own adoring audience. He began to laugh so hard at his own sick jokes that Michael Morgan couldn't stand it any longer. With a strong swipe, he cracked off his empty dip net on gunwale of the Morgan's Pride. The loud crack drowned out Black's laughter for a moment, and then Michael shouted, "SHUT DA FOOK UP! Or I'll ram this handle down yer big fook'n mouth!"

"My... My... Such brave words from a jealous man..."

"Oh... I'm not jealous of a steal'n prick like you..."

"STEAL'N! You're the one to talk about steal'n, all right!"

"That was a different thing! And you know it!"

"Steal'n is steal'n, Morgan... And I'll take da paint right off yer boat, if I could... To get you back..."

Morgan pointed the broken handle and warned, "You're not go'na get away with take'n da bread out of me family's mouth..."

Sam Black stood up, pushed out his chest, and grunted, "You didn't give a flap'n fook about my family, and I don't give a fly'n fook about yours…"

The Morgan's Pride lifted high out of the water when Michael Morgan sprung to the wharf to meet Sam Black eye to eye.

Just before the two perfect storms collided, Father John McCabe appeared from the shoreline and walked out onto the wharf. The two men parted, and Father John stepped between them. "Now lads… There's no need to be nasty between neighbors…"

Sam never saw the inside of the church, nor did he care about the cloth or the people who wore it. He stepped back for a moment, but when the dark-jacketed priest walked away from the two men, he stepped toward Michael Morgan and sarcastically sneered, "Looks like you've been saved, Morgan…" Michael knew Father John McCabe as a parish priest, but he was also a good friend of many years. Michael Morgan searched for a sign of strength from Father John and quickly found a nod of support from the good priest.

For a brief moment in time, the fog lifted, and late afternoon light gave a glimpse of bright reflections that streamed from the colorful boats. But as Father John McCabe walked back towards the shoreline, the fog quickly descended from the low-lying clouds. With every drop of heavy dew that landed upon the deck of the Morgan's Pride, the faces of Michael Morgan and Sam Black became darker. It wasn't the first time the two men had butted heads, and it wouldn't be the last. The usual tense show of accusations and insults had been a familiar sight for those who knew both men. However, on that day, Tom the bull and Uncle

Price had heard a different story coming from a darker place.

Sam Black watched Father McCabe walk to the end of the wharf, then he leaned towards Michael Morgan and mumbled, "Looks like yer savior has stranded ya…"

With a shadowed stare, Morgan responded, "I don't need protection from a shit head like you…"

Black slithered out a sick laugh and sarcastically said, "Well, you'll need a miracle to put fish in dat scow of yours…"

Morgan snapped swiftly, "Don't worry, I'll get me fish…"

Black growled back quickly, "Not if I can get it from ya…"

Michel Morgan's jaw dropped, and through clenched teeth, he said, "If you ever touches me nets again… I'll…"

Before he finished, Sam Black butted in sharply, "You'll do nut'n… Ya good for nut'n bastard…"

In the closing evening light, Tom the bull and Uncle Price could see the silhouette of Father John stoop over when Michael Morgan slowly replied, "If you tangle with me nets once more… I'll… fook'n… kill… you…"

Sam Black had made another private mark of misery, and his mission was completed for another day. He strutted out the wharf with a sickened laugh, knowing once more, he had damaged the soul of Michael Morgan. Alone in the shadowy fog, at the edge of the shore, the priest knew a darker secret. Father John stared out upon the blackened sky and recalled a confession he could never forget. He blessed himself slowly and realized, bad weather was just beginning.

Chapter 2
Upsetting Undercurrents

Sunday morning came with the smell of cooked chicken and the sound of bells tolling from the old church tower. For one day of the week, it was a time when the best clothes were dusted off, and personal differences put aside. Soaked in the soothing smell of oak pews and incense, heated discussions were not permitted to permeate the peaceful ambiance of goodwill. This unspoken rule of tolerance was acknowledged and accepted by all who attended the weekly church service in Slate Harbour. All was in complete harmony with the church protocol, until Sam Black hauled up in front of the church steps.

It only took a second for Lucy Black to get out of the truck and an instant to for her husband to see Michael Morgan in front of his rusty grill. With his truck window rolled down and his head stuck out, Sam Black shouted from the top of his lungs, "YOU'LL NEED ALL THE PRAYERS YA CAN GET, MORGAN!" Michael Morgan had been walking peacefully up the cracked concrete steps of the church with his wife and son. He kept climbing with his head down until he reached the top step and spun around. At the church entrance, Father John shuffled around the parishioners and placed himself at the side of his friend. Before Sam could respond, the good priest said, "Turn the other cheek, Mic…" Michael went to say something, but his wife Martha placed her hand on his and added, "He's not worth it…"

Mrs. Lucy Black made it to the top of the steps, and with great reluctance to meet his eyes, she added, "Don't mind him, Mic; he doesn't mean to be like that…" In the plain site of the priest and with his wife leaning against Michael Morgan, Sam Black placed his truck in low gear and screeched his tires upon the consecrated ground.

The choir conductor searched Father John McCabe for a sign to begin mass, but the priest was lost in thought at the back of the church. He remembered a time when a young Sammy Black served at the altar by his side. In his mind, it was like yesterday, that young fresh-faced boy recited Latin and poured the wine with reverence. Father John watched the waving conductor while he stumbled in his vestments to raise his arm. As the choir started singing and the procession began to move along, he recalled with a heavy heart of that young boy. He knew that young respectful Sam was dragged up through life by a disrespectful drunk. Reaching the altar, Father John McCabe blessed himself and said a silent prayer for the broken boy who became a misunderstood man.

At the end of the service, Father John waited at the back of church with rejuvenated spiritual energy. One by one, they filed out the back door to shake his hand and wish him well. Everyone left the service in peace, with the exception of one. With a tight grip of her hand and a long look from her ocean-colored eyes, Father John McCabe knew Lucy

Black wanted something more than a friendly goodbye. Father John gave Lucy a slow wink with a soft smile, and with that sign, they headed for the back pew.

They sat in silence for a moment, then he asked, "What's bothering you, my child?" It didn't take long for the loose tears to fall down upon the solid oak pew. Lucy looked at the good priest with her teal-green eyes, she sobbed, "It's Sam…"

"You know his life was hard, my dear…"

"Yes, I know, Father but now it's hard on me…"

Knowing the answer may come from a hidden place, he asked tentatively, "Why now?"

"Father, he's obsessed with destroying Michael Morgan…"

"But that's not new… They never saw eye to eye, ever since they were young boys…"

"I know, Father, but this is different… I think he knows something…"

The priest took her hand and said, "Be strong, my child… He doesn't know…" He looked up towards the ceiling and continued, "The poor man has been hardened by a tough life… Now he's chiseling away at Michael Morgan in frustration…" Lucy wiped her eyes, shook her head, and said, "No… It's something else…" Father John McCabe leaned back on the pew and sheepishly asked, "Then, what's this new concern of yours?"

"Well, Father… You know about the brief relationship I had with Michael when Sam and I parted for that short time…" Father John lifted his eyebrows, looked towards the confessional box, and slowly replied, "Yes, indeed… I do…" He blessed himself and added, "Everyone makes mistakes, my child…"

"Well, Father, now, when he drinks hard, he asks more questions than I can handle…"

She looked directly at the good priest in his forgiving eyes and pleaded, "I need help, Father John…"

Father John McCabe understood Lucy Black was at a weak point in her life. He knew his hands of healing would be expected and accepted with obedience and without question. Father John laid his hand upon Lucy's head and said, "May God give you the strength to carry on…" He made the sign of the cross over her forehead and blessed her closed eyes.

"Thank you, Father… You're the only person who knows about the cross I bear." The priest stood and whispered softly, "What happened in the confessional box will never be revealed."

Father John bid his farewell to Lucy Black and headed for solace within the confines of the silent sacristy. It was a place where he shed his vestments, and for a brief moment, the responsibilities of a parish priest. Removing his outside vestment, Father John was startled to see Martha Morgan standing in the corner of the sacristy. She stepped forward and sharply apologized, "I didn't mean to startle you, Father." Seeing soiled vestments in her hands, Father John remembered she was there to collect his wine-stained cassock. He quickly bowed and said, "Not to worry, my dear…" Under the stained-glass light of the afternoon sun, Father John could see streaks of sadness showing on her face and quickly understood there were more important things than the stains on his clothes. He waved her closer and asked, "Is there something I can help you with, my dear?" She laid the vestments on the table close by and said, "I'm worried about Michael…"

Michael Morgan had been friends with Father John for many years. From the time Michael was a boy fishing off the side of the wharf until the time he grew into a man providing for his family, he had always been friends with Michael. He knew Michael Morgan was a God-fearing man, who was carved from the salt of the seas that surrounded their rocky shores.

In the reflection of stained-glass windows, Father John had seen the strain on Martha's face. Her tension triggered him to reach out his hands and say, "Then I'm worried too…"

In the shadowed sacristy, surrounded by oak-paneled walls, they sat around the small table under the colored windows. Without encouragement, Martha began, "Father, I'm afraid what Michael is going to do…"

"Do?"

By the puzzled look upon the good priest's face, Martha Morgan continued to cast a light of concern. She said, "He's obsessed with the idea that Sam Black is steal'n da fish out of his nets…" She buried her face in her hands and sobbed through her fingers, "I think he's go'n do something very dark…"

The rays of sun pushed through the clouds and spread upon the stained-colored windows, shedding new light upon the old walls. Father John realized very quickly that old walls could crumble with the sharp words from someone's loose lips. He recalled those confessional whispers and wondered if those words had pushed his friend into a fanatical frenzy. He watched Martha Morgan carefully for a moment and then asked, "Why do you think he's so obsessed with Sam Black now?" Before she could answer, he continued, "They've been fishing in the same community for years, and it has never reached such a heated frenzy before…" The priest sat back and studied her silent response. Her honest movement and unrelenting stare suggested she had no hidden agenda. He pried for more, "Why do you think it would go to a darker place, Martha?" She looked at him straight in the eyes and said, "With cod fish so scarce, I would think it's push'n him over the edge…"

"Hmmm… Indeed…" With no hint of the hidden secret, Father John relaxed on his chair and continued, "This too will pass…" He sat up straight, made the sign of the cross, and with a returning soft smile, the load seemed lifted from the cracks of Martha Morgan's face. Father John stood up, and they walked towards the heavy wooden door. He opened it with ease, knowing on that day, there were no words of disclosure left upon the sacristy table.

Outside, there was no sign of her son Matthew. She saw him leaving when the communion bells rang just before consecration, and there was nothing she could do about it. At nineteen, Matthew was becoming a man, and that meant she needed to give him a wide berth. She tucked the soiled vestments tightly under her arm and headed to the back of the church, were Michael was waiting patiently in the truck.

"Did you see Matthew leaving during mass?"

"Yes, I saw da young bugger…"

"Where do you suppose he's gone?"

"Oh, I got a good idea…" Martha watched him push the stick hard into first gear and quickly popped the clutch. She sternly said, "It wasn't too long ago, you were a snot-faced boy on the wharf too, Michael Morgan!" He didn't crack a smile. Michael Morgan just squealed the worn tires when they hit the worn-out pavement.

Down by the wharf, where the ocean lapped the pebbled beach, Matthew Morgan and Junior Black were skimming rocks on flat water. When the church communion was about to begin, it was Matthew's cue to step out from the exit door. Every Sunday, the young men would converge on the foot of the steps and then head for cover behind the fishing stages. Down by the calm beach, Matthew and Junior could find the confidence to speak among confides of the silent stages. It was one of two places where a secret friendship was kept between the pillars of two feuding families.

In between the cracked clapboard, young Junior hauled out two warm beers. He popped two tops with an old caulking iron and asked, "Why do think our fadders don't like each other?"

Young Matthew took a swallow of his warm beer, "Maybe it's the lack of fish." Junior took a gulp and added, "Naw…. It's something else, b'y…" He picked up a rounded beach rock, flicked it in the water, and said, "Who gives a fook anyway…" Junior turned to toward Matthew, placed the beer in the air, and with a searching toast, he said, "Hey, b'y…" Matthew returned the gesture of solidarity with high-raised warm beer.

Junior took another gulp and continued, "Fadder is bit of a prick sometimes, but I'm used to his shit…" Matthew had known Junior Black since childhood, and he knew when not to add fuel to the flaming fire. Matthew did not want to cross a line he couldn't step over. He didn't want to hear about stolen fish or anything else that would put their forbidden friendship in jeopardy. Matthew tried to defuse the situation very quickly by throwing his empty bottle in the cold water with a challenge, "A buck for the first one to hit it!"

The echoes of high-pitched laughter bounced from stage to stage with each attempt to scuttle the bobbing target. Soon after the bottle sunk, settled waters returned between the two young men. As they stood and stared over the still harbor waters, Matthew threw out a sobering statement, "Me and you are a lot alike…" Junior tossed his last rock and responded, "I always thought that too…" With a grin of approval, Matthew went on, "Me and you are… like…" Matthew didn't finish his words. His father's truck came up the dirt road by the stages, spinning rocks all the way. Michael Morgan's unexpected presence pushed young Junior to scramble for cover behind the pillars that held up the fishing stages. Under a cloak of seaweed, and behind the safety of those mussel-covered pillars, young Junior watched while his friend was reluctantly swept away by his angry father.

Michael Morgan didn't spare the worn shocks or rusty springs on his old truck. He pushed the pedal down and bounced back toward the main road. The bumpy ride over the beach was short-lived, with the sight of the pavement in plain view. Back on the smooth road, they began a blind turn around an old saltbox house. With their line of sight blocked, Matthew squirmed in the seat and tried to make his father see his side of the story, "What's wrong with hang'n out on the beach?" There was no time for long-winded stories. In a panic, Michael Morgan pulled the wheel sharply to the right, avoiding a large obstacle in the middle of the road. Under a bright blue sky with sun rays streaming down, the morning had almost tragically ended with the imprint of Tom the bull upon the truck's grill. On a blind turn, directly in front of them, Tom the bull was teetering back and forth with his big belly hung out and his hands full of beer bottles. Shaken but not shocked with the sudden appearance of big Tom, Michael Morgan sat back in his seat with great relief, knowing that his rusty brake lines held. He also wasn't surprised when the man as big as a whale opened his truck door and said, "Thanks for da lift, fellers…" Without further discussion, Tom the bull entered and pushed his way into the squatty cab. Wedging Matthew between Michael and himself, he put his finger in air and slurred, "Take… Take me to da Slippery Squid pub…"

After Tom the bull was poured out at the Slippery Squid, Michael Morgan's attention quickly returned to his renegade son. He shifted gears and asked, "Why were ya hang'n with Sam Black's son?"

"We were just throw'n rocks, that's all…"

"I don't care if you were throw'n boulders!"

"Okay, we drank one beer…"

"I don't care if you drank a dozen!"

"Then what's da problem, Fadder?"

"I don't want you hang'n with Sam Black's son, that's the problem!"

Matthew remembered their conversation on board the Morgan's Pride and said, "You were going to tell me why you didn't like the cut of Mr. Black's jib, just before the hydraulic hose bust'd..." The road ahead presented two different options. One road headed home, where the pea soup would be passed without any questions. The other road led to the hill overlooking the community, where wild winds could sweep away old secrets. Michael Morgan pulled hard to the left and began to climb the difficult incline of disclosure.

Each and every house in Slate Harbour could be seen from the bluff on the hill. It was a high point for young lovers to hide at night and a lofty place where sensitive conversations could be spoken and not heard in the light of day. On the top of the hill, overlooking the sea and land, Michael put his foot on the handbrake and began to open up, "It was a long time ago, and I was only a young tom-cod like you..." He leaned back on the worn seat and continued, "Sam and Lucy had just broken up... I was down at the Slippery Squid when Lucy came in and told me she had enough of Sam's abuse..." There was a long silence, until Matthew prodded, "And what happened then, Fadder?" His father turned towards the truck window and then back at his son, "We had too many slow dances with too many beers..." He cracked the window for fresh air and said, "And well, dat night... Da tide came and went..."

"Da tide came and went? What do that mean, Fadder?"

"Do I have to spell out everything, boy?" With a long stare and a few seconds to let it sink in, an understanding slow head shake was returned by his son. Michael Morgan continued, "The next day, Sam came crawl'n back like a bloody sand crab, and Lucy went back with him like a sucker."

Young nineteen-year-old Matthew slowly rolled down his window and sucked in the salty fresh air. He flipped his head toward his father and said, "Wow… I never saw that one come'n, Fadder…"

"Well, now ya can see why he always had it in for me, Son… He never forgave Lucy and he always hated me."

"But he married her… And you married, Mudder…"

"Yes… but that was a long time ago, and there has been plenty of water pass under the Slate Harbour Bridge…"

"So… Why are you so angry with him now?"

"I knew that bastard was always steal'n from our nets, but with fish so scarce… He's take'n the food right from our table…" With a wrenched grip on the steering wheel, his faced withered in thought, as he continued, "If I catches him… I'll…" He couldn't find the soft words to say to his only son, so he watered down his response, "He'll be sorry… put it that way…"

The old Ford engine was quick to turn over with a few swift pumps of the gas pedal. Michael Morgan's signal was clear; he was done with any further discussion and ready to head downwards. For Matthew, the air seemed to be a bit clearer up on the hill, until he watched his father navigate the sharpest turn with a blank look upon his face. Taking his eyes off the winding road, Michael Morgan turned to his son and said, "Roll up da window… And keep yer big mouth shut…" With a slow crank of the window handle and a nervous stare out over the edge, Matthew quickly realized there was more to worry about than the approaching turns taken by an absent driver. He understood quite clearly that his father's tide may have come in on a drunken affair but could now go out with everything he used to know.

Chapter 3
Red-Handed

Monday morning came with the usual preparations for the regular fishing area just outside of Slate Harbour. The everyday routine included everything required to catch the elusive cod. Hauling gill nets aboard the boat hand over hand was regular procedure. Long lines of triple-braided rope were normally coiled and tossed upon the wooden deck. Finally, the usual marking buoys were flicked right on top of the nets and rope. When it was all on board, the remaining task of loading the lunch was finally handed down from the wharf to the wheelhouse. On this regular Monday morning, when the final chore of handing down the food was in place, Matthew noticed something in the food bag that wasn't normal.

"This don't feel right, Fadder!" He felt the hard item within the plastic bag and continued, "Mudder gave us the wrong bag, Fadder!" Michael Morgan stuck his head out from the wheelhouse side window and growled, "Pass that in here, and get the lunch from the truck!"

"What's it this bag?"

"Never mind what's in the bag, do what yer told!"

Without hesitation, his father latched onto the plastic bag and hauled it through the wheelhouse window. He tucked it close by his side, smiled, and whispered to himself, "We'll see who needs the prayers…" With an affectionate tap on the top of the bag, he yelled to his son at the top of his lungs, "LET ER GO, MATTY!"

The fishing ground was only a few miles outside the community of Slate Harbour.

Without putting the throttle down, the boats could leave from the wharf and reach the shallowest part of the fishing ground in thirteen minutes flat. At this short distance, the boats could come and go all day long to check the nets for fish and reposition the nets at any time of day. Normally, the fisherman would work around the three major shoals to ensure maximum benefits would be achieved.

Depending on the time of season, nets would be placed at different depths around the fishing ground. In spring, the nets would be positioned on the top of ground where the water was shallow. In summer, the nets would be positioned on the edge, midway down over the bank. In fall, the nets would be positioned at the deepest part of the ground. On that morning, as the sleepy fog rolled over the smooth waters, Michael Morgan wasn't concerned about where his nets would be positioned upon the three fishing shoals. He wasn't interested in catching codfish at all. Michael Morgan had his mind set and a new flashy gadget ready to snag a shark in the middle of someone else's big net.

It was the perfect morning to go fishing with his new technical toy. Under the dark umbrella of the low-lying fog, Michael Morgan hauled out a new instant-print camera from his old plastic bag and laid gently on the instrument panel. It was a new powerful weapon in the ongoing war with his nemesis, Sam Black. If luck was on his side that morning, he would slip under the silence of fog and snap his enemy in action. One quick picture would tell the thousand words that he had been repeating for a long time.

Matthew suspected the Morgan's Pride was not on the regular course as they came and went over good fishing ground. As time went by, his suspicion was confirmed when he looked through the wheelhouse window and noticed his father's gill net gloves were high and dry in the wheelhouse. After another regular fishing spot flashed by in their wake without turning on the net hauler, Matthew figured it was high time to check the skipper's course for the Morgan's Pride.

Matthew stepped into the cabin and caught a glimpse of the camera placed upon the control panel. He glanced at the camera and then to his father, and asked, "What's up, Fadder?"

"It's been a long time coming…"

It didn't take long before young Matthew connected the dots that led from the camera to Sam Black. He shook his head in disbelief and asked, "What are the chances you'll catch him today?"

His father looked out over the bow of the Morgan's Pride and said, "It's the perfect day for dat prick to play his tricks…"

Still shaking his head, Matthew exclaimed, "What!"

His father scanned from port to starboard and continued, "Under da cover of the fog and in these still waters with no wind, he'll make his slippery move…"

Over the loud whining sound of the John Deere engine, Matthew raised his voice to say, "He'll hear a boat coming a mile off." Michael Morgan shut the John Deere down and, with a wild grin upon his unshaven face, pointed through the rear wheelhouse window. In the echoed aftermath of the tapping engine, his startled son stared out at the aft and watched their small, towed tender swing in the soft tide. With a tip of his head to his son, he said, "He won't hear anyone today…"

On the water, with a light mist of fog hanging in the air, Michael Morgan stepped on the narrow gunwale outside the wheelhouse cabin. With rubber boots that clung to the slippery thick-painted focsle, he untied the rusty anchor. The old heavy anchor strapped on the focsle was rarely used until that strange day. Signaling to his bewildered son for help, Michael Morgan was ready to go where he never went before.

"One… Two… Three!"

The heavy anchor reluctantly lurched over the side of the boat and quickly hung up by its outstretched steel claw. Michael kicked with all his might but couldn't stir the stubborn anchor until Matthew levered it with their boat hook. Finally, with the two men tilting the long staff of the boat hook, the hesitating anchor gave in and splashed down into the deep dark waters of the cold Atlantic.

"Come on, Son, let's get in the punt."

It was a homemade tender built in the shape of an old traditional Newfoundland punt. Michael Morgan had taken the mold from their grandfather's old trap skiff, which had been left upon a sandy beach to rot. From a simple soft copper pipe, each section was carefully molded and pressed with precision upon a cardboard template. Transferred to scaled-down wooden molds, the final product resulted in a modified tender that floated proudly behind the Morgan's Pride. Michael Morgan grabbed the painter from the punt and muttered, "Get in, Son…"

"I'm not get'n in, Fadder…"

For a brief second, his father's face dropped with Matthew's muttering mutiny. He hesitated for a moment, then he pushed himself away from the Morgan's Pride and said, "Please yourself, Son."

Michael Morgan knew the fishing ground well and didn't need any fancy navigational aids to show him where to go and when to stop. He was a seasoned skipper who knew the compass and understood the signs of the sea. In a blanket of fog, skipper Morgan was fully aware that he was headed directly for the sweetest spot on the shoal. He also knew it was the spot where the recent high-liner, Buck O'Reilly, had set his nets. Pulling his oars with stealth precision, Michael Morgan was positive it was the place he'd catch Sam Black red-handed. In this prime location, under the veil of thick fog, Michael Morgan pulled in his oars and stretched out his ears over a sea of silence.

On the day before, Buck O'Reilly had returned from fishing with an unexpected load of cod. There was no way for Buck to hide his good fortune at the weigh scales when the full bursting bag was lifted high for all to see. The tantalizing catch swung back and forth under the mesmerizing sun, while all the fishermen, with the exception of one, stood and stared. Michael Morgan didn't look at the busting bag of cod swinging in broad daylight.

He had been too busy watching Sam Black's watering eyes and too occupied planning his perfect trap.

In the thick fog, Sam Black was alone and unaware of the silent punt that was soaking slowly towards him. In the boat with a broken jib, he was doing the unthinkable. Sam Black was hauling Buck O'Reilly's nets by hand and cleaning them out fist by fist. Hauling as hard and fast as he could, without the aid of noisy hydraulics or his loud diesel engine, he was making noble time while stealing the fish from another man's net. It was all working as planned, except for the sight of one silent little punt, skippered by one persistent man.

There it was straight ahead, a boat he could not mistake. In an obscurity of overcast fog, Michael Morgan could plainly see the mist upon its dark green hull. He could clearly make out the broken jib that stabbed the fog high above the stern. Michael Morgan was sure he had hit his mark when he spied the back of Sam Black's bald head glistening in the misty air.

With every fistful of net that Sam Black hauled, the cod came in with every mesh.

Michael Morgan was so close to Sam's boat, he could hear him gloat, "A face in every window… Two in some…" The excitement was boiling over from the anticipation of Sam Black catching the cod and Michael Morgan catching Sam Black.

Michael Morgan gave one hard push and hauled in his oars. The little punt slid pass the stern and onto the side of Sam Black's boat with the broken jib. It was as if Sam had expected Michael to appear from nowhere. He didn't seem startled but appeared to be calm as he clamped the net with one hand and wiped off the fish slime with the other. Before he could speak or hide the stolen catch, Michael Morgan sung out, "SMILE FOR DA CAMERA, ya slimy bastard…" In a watery world where familiar sounds of soft sea breezes embrace the ocean's bounty, an unfamiliar sound echoed across the smooth water. CLICK! The mechanical marvel of photography had just captured a stolen moment in time.

Sam Black released the fully loaded net from his tight grasp and grabbed onto the knife that was stabbed into the knee of the boat. He knew the ripples from Michael Morgan's little punt would cause him great concern. That unexpected click would open up cracks in every crevice of Slate Harbour if he didn't act dangerously fast. He pointed his rusty knife towards Michael Morgan, and from the bilge of his stomach, he cried out, "IF YOU SCUTTLES ME… I'll CUT YOU!"

Michael Morgan was beyond threats from a thief or intimation by a mortal enemy. He stood holding the gooseneck, while the soft current carried him slowly by the boat with the broken jib. Drifting side by side, the men were eye to eye and could see the reflection of a churning sea into the depth of their frozen eyes. For that single moment, it seemed both reflected back to a time when boys were boys. Back then, they threw sticks and stones without realizing that words could do more damage. Now, staring into each other's wrinkled faces at the point of a knife, both men understood the meaning of Sam's hanging words. Michael Morgan grinned, while Sam Black snapped, "I'll give you no more warnings, Morgan… If you show that picture, you'll regret it for the rest of your life." Under a brief ray of sunshine that burst through the foggy sky, Michael Morgan took the newly printed picture from the instant camera, raised it above his head, and exclaimed, "Your jib has been had, Black!"

Back on board the Morgan's Pride, Matthew waited for his father from the safety of the well-built wheelhouse. It was a boat made from the necessity of patience and the sweat that came from hard labor. Scraping and scratching for every cent, his father put everything he had into building that wooden boat. Each plank and every nail came one by one, with every drop of cash he could collect. Over time, he hacked the keel and hammered the plank with pure persistence and an unrelenting spirit. As a young boy, Matthew had watched his father build the Morgan's Pride from the dust of his pockets and toil of his brow. He gripped his hands upon the wooden wheel and looked out upon the sea of shadows for any sign of his seafaring skipper.

It was a sound he had heard on the water many times before, but this time, that everyday sound brought a wave of relief. Matthew rushed to the rail and saw his father rowing toward the Morgan's Pride with light oars and a lifted spirit. He grabbed the painter from his father and asked, "What's so funny, Fadder?" His father never replied. He hopped aboard the Morgan's Pride and said, "Let's go haul'n some hook n' line."

Matthew lashed on the painter and asked, "What happened out there in the fog?"

His father tapped his top pocket and replied, "What happens in da fog stays in da fog, till the right time, that is…"

"But did you catch anyone at the nets?"

Matthew's father gave him a half grin and replied, "A picture will tell a thousand words to the right person…" Without explaining himself, he entered the wheelhouse and said, "Let's go haul'n hooks…"

It was late spring when the gill nets were normally used, and longlines were usually kept in the stage until later in the season. Because of Buck O'Reilly's lucky strike of cod, the prime areas were peppered with numerous gill nets. Facing a scenario of wall-to-wall gill nets, Michael Morgan decided to try something different. That morning, he would try longlines of hooks out in deeper waters.

In smooth waters, it was the perfect time for hauling longlines. The longline of multiple hooks would be set fifty fathoms long and at various depths all over the fishing grounds. The lines would be baited with squid, set over the stern, and then left to soak for a short time. Based on changing weather or the expired time, they would be hauled back with the hydraulic hauler. Each hook was baited with squid and attached to the main line with a short attachment line. In perfect weather, hook and line were usually carried out without incident. However, in rough waters, it would be a different story that came with the strain of wind and the stress of danger.

Just outside the shoal fishing ground, Michael Morgan placed the shifter in neutral and stepped out onto the deck. Matthew had the buoy in his hand and ready to throw. The automatic baiter was loaded to the brim and set to run. All was ready for Michael Morgan's command. With a quick nod of approval, Matthew threw the buoy over the side and stepped back away from the sharp hooks that fired out from the baiter. At a steady speed, the clinking of the hooks from the automatic baiter dinged and pinged, until the last hook bounced and scraped its way out over the stern. There was nothing more left to do but let the hooks soak while they watched the lifting fog.

When the fishing longlines were set, dissipating fog was not necessarily a good thing, and Michael Morgan was well-aware of that reality. The seasoned skipper knew that when fog cleared out, the wind would come in with a vengeance. With only half the soaking time expired for the hook and line, Michael Morgan looked up at the wind blowing the mast wires and said to his son, "We better haul before the wind gets any stronger."

Hauling hook and line in windy weather was a dangerous business. With every whisper of wind and every hint of a breeze, the concern of safety increased. In strong winds, the Morgan's Pride required continual attention to keep the proper slack on the long line of hooks. If the line was too loose, it could tangle in the engine propeller. If too tight, it could jump the hauler and cause everyone to scramble for cover on deck. Without proper attention to the ship's wheel, sharp flying hooks from the hauler could hook and haul a person overboard in a spilt second.

The first line of hooks came aboard with some fancy wheel maneuvers by skipper Morgan. Spinning the wheel nonstop, to the right and to the left, he kept the boat up to the wind without missing a hook. Matthew quickly responded efficiently, by racking each hook as they came in fast and furious from the hydraulic hauler.

On the second line of hooks, it all fell asunder. Deep in a trance of considering Sam Black's cutting words, skipper Morgan forgot where he was and why he needed to pay attention to the wheel. Before Michael Morgan could realize, the line became too tight for the hauler to handle and then it all unraveled before his eyes.

"SHE'S AS TIGHT AS DRUM, SON!"
"SHE'S SLIP'N, FADDER!"
"STAND BACK, SON..."

At maximum strain, the trawl line jumped the hauler and started to drag out the hooks from the baiter at lightning speed. Countless sharp clinking hooks fired out at Gatling gun speed right before Matthew's eyes. For a moment, it seemed they would escape the inevitable, until the unthinkable happened. One sharp hook bounced from the baiter and struck his father's Adam's apple with a thud, and then it carried on. By pure fate, the sharp barb had hit the other way. If turned inward, it would have hauled his father out over the side by the throat. When the last hook went over the side, Michael Morgan wobbled over the deck and then laid out on top of the braided rope.

In a sea of snake-like ropes, Matthew sat down beside his father and said, "You never made that mistake before..." He looked at his son and replied, "I have plenty on my mind these days..."

"But if that hook was turned around, it would have hooked ya by the throat and hauled ya overboard!"

Michael Morgan sat up on the surrounding ropes and placed a hand on his upper pocket and said, "I wasn't worried about me throat, Son... I was worried I'd lose me chance to set things straight..."

"What's in the pocket, Father?"

His father hauled out the newly printed picture and flung in on the slithering ropes,

"AND NOW, WILL YOU BELIVE ME?"

"But…"

"No but's about it… It's captured in living color for all to see!"

On the stern of the Morgan's Pride, young Matthew stared down upon the glossy picture of evidence. He didn't respond. His father finished the conversation, "It's dat bastard, Sam Black, and he's finally caught, RED-HANDED!"

Chapter 4
Picture of Proof

It was Friday night in Slate Harbour, the busiest time of the week down at the Slippery Squid. The bar was normally filled on Fridays with tourists and local customers looking for warm conversation and cold beer. Three distinct types of customers would take over the bar in their own turn as the day moved on. Tourists would be the first to file in, followed by the fishermen, and then finally, the fresh-faced crowd would finish off the night with lively Newfoundland jigs and reels.

Early that Friday afternoon, a large group of tourists filed in for the traditional 'Screech In'. This was a long-time touristic ritual, where come-from-away mainlanders would become honorary Newfoundlanders by partaking in the Screech-in ceremony. This formal process was usually guided by a grand master of ceremony, who would normally be the owner of the Slippery Squid. The procedure would be performed with a strict protocol of continual laughter, as the tourists proceeded through each embarrassing step along the way. From reciting the Newfoundland creed to swallowing local baloney while chugging Newfoundland Screech, the whole affair guaranteed a good time for all. To cap off the ceremony with the ultimate indignation, the participant would be required to kiss the slimy cod before they received their final reward. If all the activities were preformed correctly and if everybody appeared to have a good belly laugh, the participant would be given an official document to prove they had been screeched in as an honorary Newfoundlander.

At the end of the screech-in, and while the tourists were heading out early in the evening, their seats were filled by the next round of customers, who didn't care about kissing the cod. As the last tourists filed out the door of the Slippery Squid, the locals entered and took their places at the bar and the nearby tables. Most of the early evening customers were local fishermen who came to slurp down beer and spill some local tea. Once a week, the nets and hooks were set aside for some rest and relaxation. It was a time to blow off steam at the local pub in the company of other fishermen who were all in the same situation of uncertainty.

Fishermen came in like a tidal wave, settling on stools or sitting wherever they could. Uncle Price was quick to grab a bar stool, and the first to blurt out, "Those mainlanders are lucky to have a cod to kiss, these days…" From across the bar, a crusty voice replied, "I don't know… If catches keep come'n like the one Sam Black had today… We'll be okay…" From a dark corner of the bar, a booming voice bellowed out, "Who did you say got a load of fish?"

Uncle Price placed his beer down and sputtered, "Sam Black."

The booming voice replied, "That's funny, I was the only one getting fish then, and all of a sudden, I get nut'n today, and that prick gets it all?"

Uncle Price took a slow sip of beer and said, "Smells fishy to me…"

Buck O'Reilly stepped into the light, and with his big presence and booming voice, he replied, "That's more than fishy… That stinks to high heaven…" Buck O'Reilly waved to his buddies, and then they headed towards a table under the hanging light.

Slate Harbour was a small community, where the houses were in close quarters and everybody's whereabouts were in clear view. Built side by side, their homes were packed in like sardines around the tiny harbor. From the big concrete steps of the church to steel bar stools of the club, it was all within a short walking distance. This close proximity for certain residents had its good points and its bad, depending on the perspective of the person. For those who lived next to the Slippery Squid, it was a convenient short walk of shame when they had one too many. For those who lived next to the Slippery Squid and were members of the church, the notion of having a line-of-sight view from the priest's house was not necessarily an advantage. In this case, the parish priest had a front-row seat and could easily see who came and went at the Slippery Squid.

On that Friday night, with an earful of Martha Morgan's words replaying in his mind, Father John McCabe could clearly see from his front-row seat across the road that a good soul had slipped. The priest swiftly stood to attention and doubled-checked through the hanging drapes. Yes, it was a close friend who could easily fall from grace behind the big doors of the Slippery Squid.

Michael Morgan was on a specific mission when he stepped into the Slippery Squid pub.

He wasn't a regular to the bar, but from time to time, he would visit for special occasions.

During those rear visits, smiles were never scarce for Michael when he entered the Slippery Squid doors. No matter when or what time he decided to visit, there was plenty of friendly fishermen ready to shake his hand and buy him a cold beer. Michael Morgan was, indeed, a well-liked man who had gained the respect of his fellow fishermen and surrounding community.

Sam Black slipped through the door of the Slippery Squid without fanfare. There were no sunny smiles from the crowd, nor offers of free beer. He was a regular at the bar, and it was normal for the other fishermen to ignore his presence with cold shoulders and turned backs. The sight of him would instigate subtle warnings of strained coughs and shifting chairs, followed by shifting eyes and silent sneers. Needless to say, Sam Black's dark presence brought unwelcome gestures from every corner of the Slippery Squid.

At opposite sides of the bar, Morgan and Black could clearly see each other's shady silhouettes. Michael Morgan noted his aggressive stance from a distance but turned his back and headed towards the friendly table under the hanging lamp.

"Any room for me over here?"

With a big broad smile, Buck O'Reilly replied, "Sit down, ya fool…"

Michael Morgan tapped the boys on their back and grabbed an empty seat alongside Buck O'Reilly. Under the bright light of the hanging lamp, he said, "Don't mind if I do…"

"Yer a site for sore eyes around this dump, Mic..." Buck placed one of his beers in front of Michael and asked, "What brings a church-go'n man in here today?"

"I thought I'd enlighten you..."

Buck looked around the table of smiling faces and replied, "We could use a few prayers in here... Hey, b'ys!"

Buck O'Reilly was built like a bull moose and wasn't the type of guy to make a fool of. Buck had a short fuse that could be lit by the wrong word from the right guy. Uncle Price always stated, "If Buck had antlers, they'd tag him in da fall, for a moose!" With the slightest push, Buck O'Reilly would butt anyone with his big thick head and plow them into the ground in a blink. In the context of his quick temper, all chairs tipped back when Buck's smile dropped, and he asked, "What are ya really here for, Mic?"

Michael Morgan knew his friend Buck extremely well. He had grown up with him since they were young boys in their small outport community. Michael was well-aware of his good friend's bad temper, but he was not afraid of him. He knew Buck O'Reilly would never turn on him, no matter what the circumstance.

Ten years back, Buck O'Reilly had a turn of luck that found him in deep trouble. Busted, broken, and laying in a pool of blood in the bush, Buck had accidently shot himself while hunting. It was Michael Morgan who found him and tied a torniquet on his leg. Two miles on, Michael Morgan carried his friend upon his back. He trudged on through the marsh and the muck until he had his friend Buck O'Reilly on safe ground.

With his question hanging in the air, Buck O'Reilly reached out his big hand and said, "There's nut'n you can say to get me angry… Nut'n."

Michael Morgan shook his hand and said, "I'm not worried about myself…"

"Who are ya worried about, Mic?"

From a dimly lit corner, Sam Black stepped out and walked towards the table under the hanging light. With the conversation cut short, Buck O'Reilly turned towards Black and growled, "What da fook do you want?"

No words were spoken by Sam Black. He passed the table and made a slicing motion on his throat while looking straight at Michael Morgan. Black continued on towards the toilets and disappeared down the long dark hall.

Buck O'Reilly put his hand on his friend's shoulder and asked, "Is that prick bothering you? 'Cause if he is, I'll…"

Michael Morgan quickly interrupted and said, "No… No, he hasn't bothered ME… This time…"

Around the table, sat fishermen who were all going through the same hard times of empty nets. Even though Buck O'Reilly had experienced a short period of hauling full nets, they knew the cod fishery was falling fast. From the other side of the table, Tom the bull spoke up, "It looked good there for a while, Buck…" Uncle Price added, "But she's gone now…" Buck O'Reilly shook his head in disbelief, placed his opened hands upon the table and said, "It don't make any sense…"

Uncle Price and Tom the bull were ready to pump up the pressure from the other side of the table. They knew Buck would pounce like a spring if they wound him tight enough.

"I told ya it was fishy…"

"More than fishy, it stinks."

"There's something else on the go…"

"I know, but nobody seems to know what it is…"

Inside Buck O'Reilly the steam began to build, with every spoken hint that the two men spouted. His deep brown eyes darted from man to man with every innuendo, while his fists began to tighten with every insinuation. He looked up at Sam Black, who had resumed his position on a stool in the darkened corner at the end of the bar. Without warning, Buck struck the table hard. His flying fist startled his friends and rattled every beer bottle that was placed upon the table.

"ENOUGH!"

Silence fell upon the table with the hanging light and finally rippled across the floor of the Slippery Squid. He stood up and finished with a challenge, "GIVE ME SOME REAL PROOF!"

Michael Morgan hung his head down, put his hand in his top pocket, and then placed the picture underneath the hanging light. In bold color, with the light bouncing off a glossy image, that picture of proof was enough to light Buck O'Reilly's fiery fuse.

In the small community of Slate Harbour, it was common knowledge that Buck O'Reilly and Sam Black hated the ground each other walked on. Everyone knew, it was only a matter of time that they would lock horns like two big angry bucks. Under the hanging light of the well-lit table, the picture was crystal clear, that a battle was beginning with the flaring of nostrils and the pawing of feet.

The room quickly became a circular centrifuge, sending a crowd of onlookers quickly to the sides for safety. Spinning in motion with the room, Buck O'Reilly searched for solid footing as he moved forward towards the darkest part of the bar. In the corner of bar was a wild-eyed man who had been hardened by the wilderness. With a loose grip around a concealed broken bottle, he was more than ready for Buck O'Reilly.

Tom the bull had seen Sam Black in action many times and knew all his dirty tricks. He had been known to strike quick and dirty, before anyone could have a chance. Tom the bull figured out quickly that Black would play the rotten card he had behind his big hairy back. Under the cover of the shadows, Tom the bull maneuvered around the spinning room until he was ready at arm's reach.

Buck O'Reilly stood in front of the shadowed Black and growled, "Yer fooked now…" Sam Black stepped out under the lights of the bar. With a dirty grin on his face, he flashed the broken bottle he had hidden behind his back and grumbled, "No… Yer fooked…"

Tom the bull and everyone else knew that right was right, and the sight of a broken bottle in front of an empty-handed man was wrong. For the sake of justice, he took a folding chair and busted it across Sam Black's broad back with one smack. Black fell to the floor, and the broken bottle slipped from his slimly hand. With the floor leveled, Tom the bull stepped back to the side and said, "Now, we'll see who's fooked…"

Buck O'Reilly was beyond angry. He was foaming from the mouth and fuming from the nostrils at the thought of being sliced open by a dirty rodent. Cornered like a wounded rat, Buck O'Reilly was aware that Black could still lash out like a wild beast from any angle. He did not give him the chance to pounce.

The first kick from Buck O'Reilly's steel-toed boot knocked Black's head back. The second kick knocked his head to the side. Buck lifted his own heavy weight and came down upon Black's chest with full extension of his leg and boot. The routine continued without letup until Sam Black was bloodied beyond recognition.

In a time when the lowest thing a man could do was rob the fish from another man's net, nobody felt pity or stepped in to help Sam Black. Buck O'Reilly kept hammering away until he finally took a break to regain his wind for the second round. With a quick sip of beer from the bar, Buck raised his fist again but was stopped by a meek voice that came from the opened door.

"He had enough, Buck..." Buck O'Reilly was not a religious man, but the sight of Father John McCabe stopped him dead in his tracks. Exhausted, he stepped back and said, "He took from me, so I gave it to him..."

Father John looked at the tortured face of Sam Black and replied, "He has paid enough for his sins..."

Buck O'Reilly straightened his back and stretched his arms while the priest watched the blood drip to the floor. Eager to finish something he had started, he sternly suggested, "Why don't you go back to church, and let me give Black his penance!"

Father John stepped up closer to Buck O'Reilly and softly said, "Everyone deserves a second chance... Don't they, Michael?"

From the sidelines, Michael Morgan stepped out from the crowd and replied, "This cut goes deeper, Father John." Buck O'Reilly stepped back when Michael picked up the broken bottle and walked toward the beaten man. Sam lifted his head, spit out a sliver of blood, and spewed, "You don't have da guts, Morgan..." Father John could taste the tension between his friend Michael Morgan and Sam Black. His worst fear was materializing right before his eyes when his good friend lifted the broken bottle in front of Sam Black's tattered face. With a swoop of his arm, the broken bottle flew through the thick air and crashed upon the barroom floor.

"It's over, Sam..."

"Nut'n is over..."

"Let's walk away from this and start a new story..."

"The only story I want to read is the news of your death..."

Buck O'Reilly couldn't resist the opportunity to land another kick. He sent Sam Black's head back to the floor with the taste of leather from his steel-toed boot. Father John McCabe stepped in before O'Reilly could change his stance and declared, "Enough blood has been shed!" He signaled to Tom the bull and Uncle Price to take the broken body off the barroom floor. As they dragged Black through the door, he broke their grasp, stood up, and gave his final stand, "I'll tell you this, Morgan..." He wiped the blood from his eyes and continued, "You'll pay for this, you prick..." Buck O'Reilly piped in before Michael could respond, "Like you paid for this picture… You prick!" With the picture of his red-handed deed swinging in Buck's hand, Black turned his back and hobbled out the door.

Father John laid his hands upon Michael's shoulders and said, "You did the right thing, my friend, by stepping away."

"He had it coming, Father…"

"Everyone needs a lesson in life sometimes…"

"Yes, but I wonder what sort of lesson Black has in mind…"

From behind the bar, a bartender shouted, "Okay b'ys, yer entertainment is over… Now, clean up this mess and let's get down to drink'n again!" Father John took his cue, and before he walked off, he asked, "Why don't you come with me, Mic?"

"I'm stay'n, Father John… I need to blow off some steam tonight…"

Father John nodded his head and then gave Michael his last words, "Where there's steam, there's a fire smoldering somewhere…"

Chapter 5
Stage of Smoke

Long after the tourists and fishermen had left the Slippery Squid, a wave of fresh-faced customers came and settled into their well-worn seats. It was the time of evening when young folks came in to loosen up and dance the lively Newfoundland jigs and reels. Under the dim lights of Slippery Squid, the young men and women of Slate Harbour would party until the sun came up over the shining sea.

Michael Morgan had not been down at the Slippery Squid for a very long time. Years ago, when he was a younger man, he was a regular customer when the fishermen left, and the jigs and reels began. But on that Friday night, without the blessing of Father John McCabe, Michael wanted to stay for the third round of customers who gathered for the late-night dance. Michael Morgan intended on staying and drowning his sinking thoughts at the bottom of a tall glass.

Numbed from watching Buck O'Reilly beating Sam Black, he sat in silence, licking the wounds of his new reality. With Sam Black's last words of revenge ringing in his mind, he clearly understood that the battle was only beginning. In the midst of his mind-bending mayhem,

Michael Morgan leaned back and sucked down a stiff drink without noticing the woman with strong-smelling perfume. She came up from behind, put her hands over his eyes, and said, "Take it easy, big boy… We have all night…"

Michael placed his empty glass down, took a long whiff of perfume, and replied, "What are ya at, Maggie?"

She removed her red glossy nails from his eyes and retorted, "Never mind me… What are you do'n here tonight, Mic?"

"Just blow'n off steam, Maggie…"

"Well, I wouldn't mind blow'n off some myself…"

Maggie Murphy caught the bartender's eye and shouted, "Give Mic a tall glass of rum, with a bucket of ice to cool him down…" The bartender gave her a half-way grin, placed the two glasses of rum in front of them, and said, "I'll start you a tab, Maggie."

"You do that, Reggie… I think it's going to be a long night…"

Michael Morgan took a long whiff of lingering perfume, grabbed his drink, and said, "I didn't come here look'n for fun tonight."

She circled the rim on the glass with her red-painted nails, slanted her head to side, and said, "The night is long, and I can wait …"

Maggie Murphy was an old fish from the past, trying to swim with a young school of fresh fish. Reality placed Maggie around Michael Morgan's age, but fantasy had stopped her hands of time. Locked in a time warp of wrinkles and regrets, Maggie Murphy felt rejuvenated with the presence of an old boyfriend from the past, who had appeared from nowhere at the end of the bar. She took a glossy sip and said, "Why don't you give me a chance tonight…"

"It was a mistake to stay here…"

"You didn't think it was a mistake back in the day, Mic…" Under the bar light, Michael could see the cracks in Maggie's caked mask. Placing herself in the shadow, she blocked his view and said, "The last time you were here at a dance, you were hot and heavy for Lucy…" He placed his finger in the ice cubes and spun them around as he searched for the closest exit door.

Maggie moved in closer, knowing she had hit a sensitive nerve of the past.

Between jigs and reels, the bar quickly filled to capacity with the young men and women of Slate Harbour. In no time at all, they were squeezed in every corner and crevice like canned sardines. It appeared the atmosphere of the Slippery Squid was fully charged and ready for a great night of close contact. However, one young man at a dimly lit table across from the bar didn't seem too enchanted by the promise of close encounter.

Young Matthew Morgan was not impressed when he saw his father sitting stool to stool alongside Maggie Murphy. Everyone in the bar had seen Maggie snag many stray men countless times with her captivating net. When floundering fishermen were at their weakest, she would pile on the perfume and pour out the liquor until they were filled to the gills. Matthew had heard the stories from far and wide and even read about it on the Slippery Squid's bathroom walls. From across the room, his father looked like a fish out of water that was ready to be filleted by experienced hands. Junior Black nudged Matthew and said, "The crowd is coming in fast and furious tonight, old bud." Matthew pointed towards his father and replied, "That's not the only thing come'n in fast tonight…"

Junior took a quick look through the crowd, sat back on his seat, and said, "Oh… That's something you don't see every day."

"Ya… Looks like me fadder's tide maybe come'n in… And may go out, tonight…"

Junior screwed up his face and said, "Whaaaaa?"

"Never mind…"

The band began to play their fine-tuned fiddles, and the dust started to fly from the two-toned floors of the Slippery Squid. It was time to pick up the rubber boots and lay them down hard, while they danced like wild salmon in a school of complete madness. Between the thumping of boots on the floor and the grinding of hips at the bar, it all became very unhinged until Father McCabe burst through the swinging doors of the Slippery Squid and cried out:

"THERE'S SMOKE… ON THE WATER!"

In an instant, the fire of passion was doused, and the dancing fever diminished. The thought of fire down on the waterfront placed a damper on the Slippery Squid dance and sent them running as fast as they could towards the harbor. There was no time to delay because everyone knew in their tight-knit community that all the houses were dangerously close.

Michael Morgan reached the bend in the road and couldn't believe his sky-blue eyes. Straight ahead, under the bright full moon was a terrible sight he could never imagine.

The flames were out of control and flicking high above his beloved fishing stage. Held high by strong wooden pillars, those stages had kept back the pounding North Atlantic waves and the fierce northerly wind. Four generations of Morgans had fished from those shaky stages, and now, right before his eyes, it was all going up in bellows of smoke.

In minutes, everyone had heard the call and came without hesitation to the assistance of their neighbor. No need of long-winded invitations; they all understood what each and every one had to do when the fire call came. If life or limb was in peril by the sea, everything would be sacrificed to save their neighboring souls. With only sticks and stones at risk this time, they stepped down and watched while fire engulfed the Morgan fishing stages.

From the crowd that arched around the beach, Father McCabe moved to the front and said sternly, "Stand back… Don't risk yer lives…"

Michael Morgan took his place in front and supported Father John with a discouraging, "Let er burn, b'ys… There's nobody at risk of dying."

Young Junior Black couldn't help himself. Like his father, Sam Black, he didn't know when to shut his mouth even at the worst times. From the crowd, his familiar voice shouted:

"WHY DON'T YA PUT OUT THE FIRE WITH OLD MAGGIE!"

Michael Morgan knew the voice and where it was coming from. He quickly waded through the crowd and grabbed young Junior by the collar, shook him and said,

"You're just like yer useless fadder…" For a moment, he stared into Junior's sky-blue eyes, and then he pushed him back. Father John was quick to reach his arm and say, "He's only a boy, Mic, leave him be…"

In the warmth of the heat and the light of the fire, Michael Morgan turned to watch his crumbling walls fall into the cold water. From the reflected watery image, he followed the lifting smoke up to the clearing on top of the hill. Under the light of the full moon, Michael Morgan could definitely see a familiar truck with a distinctive mark.

In his idling truck, Sam Black looked down upon the crowd with two bloodied eyes and a broken headlight. The view from the hill was breathtaking on a summer day when the bright blue sky blended with the crisp evergreen trees, but on that night, as the glow from the fire lit up the blackened sky, the view should have been devastating. Yet, Sam Black peered down at the gravity of the situation with a smile smeared upon his busted face. From afar, Michael Morgan had no doubt in his mind that Sam Black had lit the fire but not enough proof to take him down. Soaked in a sea of smoke, Michael could no longer look up at the root of his smoking situation. His bellowing thoughts and his churning mind were beyond rhyme or reason, from the smell of the scorched ashes and sight of his seared dream.

In the morning, the devastation for Michael Morgan was displayed under the clear blue skies. Nothing but bald rocks were seen after the tide came in and took the ashes out to sea.

There was no sign of the old fish flake that stood by the side of a stage that lasted for years. Everything was gone except an ancient cod liver oil barrel that bobbed up and down against the pulling current and a tethered rope from the resisting shore.

Michael didn't give his son Matthew much time to talk about the fire or his night at the Slippery Squid. He hauled in the cod liver oil barrel and said, "We're lucky; our nets were on this Government wharf and out of the line of fire."

Matthew didn't look at the cod liver barrel. Instead, he said, "But Fadder, the pot-bellied stove wasn't lit..."

His father didn't answer. He pointed towards their boat tied to the mooring in the bay and said, "We're fortunate. The Morgan's Pride was out of harm's way, out on the collar." Matthew didn't look at the Morgan's Pride. Instead, he said, "But Fadder, there was no oil and no gas in da stage last night..."

His father didn't answer. He pointed towards their pile of rope coiled up on the beachhead and said, "We're very lucky. The rope is not charred or damaged in any way..." Matthew didn't look at the rope. He stepped in front of his avoiding father and asked with a puzzled look, "But Fadder, there was no reason for the fire to start..."

His father stared him straight into his eyes and said, "You're right, there's no reason for our stage to go up in flames." He grabbed his son's shoulders and continued, "But nobody got hurt, and for that, we're blessed..."

Matthew nodded his head and took the peaceful opportunity to push his luck. He tilted his head and asked, "Were you blessed when the tide came in and the tide went out, with Maggie Murphy last night?" His father didn't get angry. He softly sat on the side of the wharf and said, "I may have had too many beers last night, but I never lost my mind, Son..." Matthew sat down beside his father on the wharf and watched a gull perch upon the pillar of their burnt stage. His father never looked toward the gull or the burnt stage. He stared at his son and continued, "The only tide that will come in for me is your Mudder… And she'll be the only one I'll be with until the tide goes out when I'm dead and gone." With the smell of burnt wood in the air, Matthew placed a simmering smile on his shining face. His father stood, looked out at the Morgan's Pride, and said, "We'll be alright, Son… It's only sticks and stones…" Matthew never looked towards their boat or back at his father. He was too busy watching a familiar truck with a broken headlight, hauling up at the head of the Government wharf.

Before Sam Black and his son got out of the truck, Michael Morgan walked over and said, "Why don't you get the fook out of here!" With the truck door wide open, Sam Black sarcastically responded, "Look… Let's get one thing straight… You don't like me, and I don't like you…" He stepped out onto the wharf and finished, "But I didn't burn yer fook'n fish'n stage…"

In broad daylight, Sam Black could barely see out of his blackened eyes. He was black and blue from head to toe, but Michael Morgan could easily see a lie through his busted grin. Through slippery slits for eyes, Sam watched Michael move to the rear of the truck and peer over the side. He slipped back into the truck, slammed the door shut, and said, "It got pretty hot and heavy at the Slippery Squid last night, I heard." With no response, Sam continued to stoke Michael's fire. "Junior told me it got really hot between you and dat whore Maggie Murphy too…" It took every bit of Michael Morgan's patience to keep him from losing his cool against Sam Black's spewing blast of stale air. Without succeeding in pushing Michael Morgan, Sam Black dug deep behind the seat and reached for something that would place them on even terms.

For a second, Sam seemed to change his angry rhetoric as he looked over at the scorched stage across from the Government wharf and said, "What a pity, Morgan… And it meant so much to your family…" Michael Morgan had seen the gas can in the back of his truck and knew his empty act of condolence was fake. He didn't mince words when he asked, "Why don't you fook off somewhere else, Black?" Sam Black chuckled and responded, "Now, that's no way to treat a fellow fisherman…" Still trying to portray a fake sense of concern with his phony facade, Sam Black asked, "Why don't you stand in front of the scorched stage?" Normally, Michael Morgan could smell a rotten rat from a mile away, but this time, he didn't see Sam Black's sneaky trap. With his hands full of nets and his mind full of lost memories, Michael Morgan placed a puzzled look upon his face and asked, "What do you want me to do?" Sam Black stepped out from his truck and placed an instant camera up to his blackened eye and said, "Smile for the camera, fook face!" With quick snap, he slipped back into the truck and shouted through the opened window, "I'll pin that one up at the Slippery Squid." That unexpected click cracked the pretense of concern and pushed Michael Morgan over the edge of his patience.

Morgan grabbed Black by the coat and tried to haul him out through the window with all his might. Without success, the truck door handle was fumbled and found. In seconds, the two men went rolling out the wharf, throwing punches left and right as hard as they could. Up and down the wharf they went, giving smack for smack while blindly balancing the narrow boundaries of the Government wharf.

The nasty encounter caught the attention of one curious son who happened to be in the adjacent fishing stage and heard the commotion. Junior Black was never privy to his father's dark plan for Michael Morgan. Sam Black kept him in the dark and didn't include him when he went into the deeper waters of deception. Junior was also unaware of his father's early morning net piracy or the possibility that he torched Michael Morgan's prized fishing stage. At that moment, with the familiar heated sounds hanging in the air, he knew his father was in hot water again with Michael Morgan.

Junior rushed over to the Government wharf and quickly took a stand by the side of his forbidden friend Matthew Morgan. Their eyes met, and without a spoken word, they knew where each stood while they watched their fathers' flying fists. Both young men weren't shocked and knew how deep the rift went between Michael Morgan and Sam Black. It was just another foggy day in Slate Harbour where Morgan and Black were at each other's throats under a blanket of damp blindness.

In between the punches, Junior Black asked, "What got 'em go'n this time?" Matthew pointed and replied, "Fadder thinks he burnt our stage." Junior looked at the blackened mess and said, "I know he done some shitty things, but he wouldn't stoop that low..." Matthew watched the two warriors coming closer, shook his head, and replied, "I don't know this time, Junior... I think..." Without paying attention, the sons didn't realize how close the fight had become. In a split second, Sam Black accidently struck his son with an elbow and sent him over the Government wharf with his oil skins streaming.

Junior Black couldn't swim, and the restriction of his oil skins exacerbated the dire situation to the point it was do or die. Without hesitation, Matthew jumped over the wharf, and in seconds he had his friend by the back of the neck, hauling him to the beach with strong steady strokes. In the commotion of a drowning man, Morgan and Black placed a pause on their battle and bolted for the beach.

The young men were spitting out saltwater when everyone reached the beach and gathered around. With the taste of saltwater burning his lips, Junior quivered, "I… I, was gone, b'y… I couldn't swim a stroke to save myself." Matthew coughed, pointed toward Junior's wet suit, and replied, "If you didn't have those oil skins on, you would have been fine…"

"No, b'y… You saved my life."

In a red-faced fit of anger, Sam Black pointed at Michael Morgan and growled, "Nobody would have saved anyone if yer fadder hadn't pushed him!"

In a place where peace and reconciliation could be easily found from the rescue of his drowning boy, Sam Black refused to see the opportunity of peace. He dug his rubber boots into the dark beach sand and said, "Let's get the fook out of here, Junior!" Michael Morgan went to the side of his son and tried to bring some sense to a senseless situation, "You almost lost yer son… Why don't we bury the hatchet here and go our way in peace?"

Sam Black grabbed young Junior by the arm and clenched his teeth. "If my boy had drowned, I would have buried a hatchet in yer fook'n back and burned ya in yer beds…"

No more words were needed. On that clear blue sky day, Sam Black made his perverse point crystal clear to the Morgan family. In the wake of the sickening state, Michael Morgan looked at his son, shook his head, and despairingly said, "I don't' know, Son…" In his dripping clothes, Matthew watched the truck with a broken headlight drive out the Government wharf with a tormented son. He looked at his father and added, "He's a twisted man, Fadder… And I know, this ain't go'na end well…"

Chapter 6
Ghosts of Greed

The fishing stage ashes were cleared, and life continued under a cloudy haze of deep suspicion. Michael Morgan couldn't forget Black's hatchet threat that hung over his head and couldn't forgive himself for not handling it a different way. "I should have, and I could have," rolled in and out his mind, like the waves that broke upon their rocky shoreline. It was an endless motion of disturbing thoughts that churned currents of revenge and ruthless retribution, until the winds of change blew in a greedy opportunity from a cod fishery of the past.

Somewhere in the rough waters of his mind, Michael Morgan finally found solace with the temporary return of the elusive cod. For some unknown reason, the slippery cod had slipped back into the bays in large schools for the first time in many years. There was cod fish in every corner of the bay, and it was looking to be one of the best fishing seasons ever until an untimely union strike overshadowed the potential of a good fishery.

In the midst of a migratory wonder, the threat of an all-out fishing strike placed a dagger of uncertainly into the minds of all fishermen. With the everyday union rhetoric spewing from the radio, their hope of having a good fishing season sunk like a stone to the bottom of the sea. Finally, when the union and fish plant owners walked away from the negotiation table without an agreement, the fishermen were left to fend for themselves without the possibility of selling fresh fish.

The times of load-and-go were not to be. Now, the only remaining chance of salvaging the fishing season was hung upon the flakes of the past. Years ago, the convenience of selling whole fish was not a choice. The only way of selling fish in the past was in the age-old salt fish industry. Fishermen had to split, salt, and dry the fish on fishing flakes. It was done in every community and seen all over the Island. Faced with the collapse of the fresh fish market due to the fishery strike, those rickety wooden fishing flakes would once again hold the salted fish and their hopes of survival. Pulled by the union's agenda for power and pushed by the necessity of earning a meager wage, there was no recourse but to turn their backs on selling fresh fish and look backward to hard labor that came with the heavy work of salting fish.

Salted cod required the laborious task of splitting, cleaning, salting, and drying the fish. Fishermen started their mornings in dark fishing stages, preparing the gear and then ended their day soaking their catch in heavy-handed salt. From splitting the fish on the first day to drying on the third day, it was a never-ending process of back-breaking work from sunrise to sunset.

Michael Morgan knew all about the salt fish trade and understood the ramifications of dealing with merchant ghosts of the past. In a time when there was only one outlet of selling fish, the fish merchants bought and sold with a heavy-handed approach. It had been years ago, but Michael heard the heartless stories that were passed down by family and friends. He was only a boy when their rule had ended, but old enough to know of their ruthless reign over helpless fishermen. With only one option to sell their fish, the salt fish merchants had a monopoly of greed spurred on by the quest for power over desperate people. In the shadow of the union strike, Michael Morgan knew consequences of dealing with fish merchants of the past, but he also understood the repercussions of a dim future without the possibility of selling their catch. Faced with the prospect of having a long cold winter without money, Michael Morgan knew selling to the fish merchant was the only option available.

During years of the salt fish industry, fish merchants positioned themselves in every major fishing harbor around Newfoundland. At the center point of perfect accessibly, they were within arm's reach of the raw product and adjacent to water, where deep-keeled schooners could load and go. Back in those times, with the flow of endless codfish from the teaming waters, numerous fishing merchants were needed to meet the demand. In a place where the codfish was king, they were a monarchy of merchants that ruled over the fishermen with tight fists and hardhanded greed. Reluctantly, even though the fishermen understood they were treated unfairly, they bowed down under the cold merchant's boot. Fishermen knew merchants were the only avenue for any kind of revenue in their isolated communities. Under a tight grip of the past, Michael

Morgan sat nervously in his kitchen and said softly, "This won't be easy, Martha."

"We've seen rougher waters than this, Mic…"

"But not with that God-damn merchant stick'n his hands in our pockets…"

"Maybe old Dan Ryan has changed?"

"Those pricks never change… They're blood-suck'n bastards who would cut their mudder for a buck…"

"Why don't you take your fish to a different merchant?"

"He's the only merchant prick, left buying and selling salt fish… And that's not good!"

"Maybe the fishing season will be salvaged… Maybe the strike will be over, and we won't have to bring our fish to him…"

"That's one too many maybes for me…" Michael pulled over the laced curtain and peered out from their old window. He looked down at the Morgan's Pride floating high on water and finished, "All I know is… With this union strike, we can't sell our fresh fish and the only option is to salt and sell to Dan Ryan." Martha laid a hot cup of tea in front of her husband and said, "Looks like we're fook'd, Michael Morgan…"

One week later, the fresh fish market was shut down solid by the strike. In a state of panic, the fishermen in Slate Harbour schooled around Michael Morgan's truck and began to chat. Michael turned off his truck radio and asked, "Isn't that something? Here we are with the bay filled with codfish for the first time in years and we can't sell a fook'n thing…"

Tom the bull spoke up, "We still have one sharp hook left to fish!"

Michael knew Tom the bull's response, but he wanted to hear it out loud. He nodded his head while he sarcastically asked, "Now what would that sharper hook be, Tom?" Tom the bull proudly responded, "We always got the salt fishery to fall back on!"

Michael Morgan shook his head and exclaimed, "You were still shit'n yellow when that fishery was on the go, b'y! You wouldn't know how cut-throat those merchants really were… They'd blunt a fisherman's hook with one look of their stone-cold eyes…"

Tom the bull stepped back and then gingerly said, "But times have changed, and Dan Ryan could be different now… than back in the day." Michael Morgan opened his truck door and sat inside. He fumbled for the keys, and when he found them, he looked at Tom the bull and said, "Dan Ryan is like those killer sharks, Tommy b'y… When they draw blood once, they'll never stop…" Buck O'Reilly leaned in the passenger side window and asked, "What do you think will happen, Mic?" Michael Morgan pushed his keys into the ignition and replied, "We'll fish like we have done for years. Then, we'll bring our catch in and prepare it as salt fish, just like they done in the past. Like our ancestors before, we'll dry it, day and night, and load it aboard our trucks. When all the blood, sweat and toil is done… We'll take it in the fall to merchant Dan Ryan, looking for a fair price and …" Michael Morgan put his head down and went silent. Eager to hear more, Buck O'Reilly put a grasp on the door with his big hand and asked sincerely, "And what, Mic? And what will happen when we go look'n for a fair price?"

Michael Morgan lifted his head, turned the ignition, and replied, "And we'll get cornholed by a fish merchant... Just like they did years ago..."

Later, when the fishing season opened without the fresh fish market, the salt fishery began in full swing. Unlike the fresh fishery, where the catch would be bought and sold every day at the plant, the buying selling of salt fish only occurred at the end of season. All summer, the fish would be caught, cleaned, salted, dried, and stored until and early fall, when it would be brought to the fish merchant for sale. At that time, the merchant would inspect the catch looking for insignificant flaws that would intentionally drop the price substantially. Michael Morgan was well-aware of the bleak prospects that they faced in the fall when left in the hands of the merchants. He also knew the fishing season had just begun, and that meant, it wasn't a time to weigh up fish that wouldn't be counted in the fall.

When the fishing season finally started, everyone in Slate Harbour had their head down, mending nets while minding their own business. There was no time for fighting when every minute was occupied by the laborious task of preparing salt fish. Even the Morgan and Black feud was placed on the back burner while they focused on maximizing every inch of the salty cod. For those two fighting fishermen, their festering feud would not be forgotten. Everyone in Slate Harbour were confident that when the union strike concluded, they wound continue to lock their horns of contention.

It had been a long time since the locals had seen such bountiful catches of big beautiful cod. It was load and go in Slate Harbour. Every boat came and went from the wharf with a continual cycle of catches filled to the hatches. It appeared the fish had finally come back in the right bay, but unfortunately, with the union strike, it was at the wrong time.

In the heat of summer and under the hold of a union shrike, emotions became edgy. Young Matthew began to prong the fish up on the old stage, and before he broke a sweat, his father shouted, "DON'T PRONG THE FISH THROUGH DA GUT!" Matthew wasn't accustomed to pronging up fish one by one. He was too young to know anything about the prong and too frustrated to care. He had come into a fishery where fish was hoisted with an electric winch supplied by the fresh-fish buyer. The nearby fresh fish plants had removed the task of pronging fish many years before, but now unfortunately for Matthew it was back. Every single fish had to be carefully pronged out of the boat with a pitchfork they called a prong. Matthew stood in the fish hold with his old-fashioned prong and shouted back, "WHERE AM I SUPPOSED TO PRONG DA BLOODY FISH, FADDER?" From the wheelhouse, Michael Morgan pointed towards his own head and shouted, "IN DA GOD DAMNED HEAD!" He stepped out on the deck and explained, "The fish has to be perfect, with no prong holes in the body or the fish merchant will grade it West-Indies, and we'll get nut'n for it…"

"What da fook is West-Indies, Fadder?"

"West-Indies is how they'll cornhole us if da fook'n fish ain't perfect! Now shut yer mouth and prong it in da head while I talk with Uncle Price…"

Uncle Price and Tom the bull arrived at the Morgan's new stage and sat in the shade of the gutting table. Michael climbed up on the wharf and asked, "How did the other boats do?"

"All had fish, right to da gunwales…"

Michael Morgan removed his cap, scratched his head, and sat down beside the two men. He placed his cap back on, and in frustration he responded, "What da fook is the good of all this fish when that greedy merchant bastard is going to give us nut'n for it?"

Uncle Price had been there when the salt fish trade was in full swing. As a young man, he had seen many fishermen place their heavy loads of perfect salt fish at the feet of merchants, only to receive the lowest price. Neither the sweat from their brows nor the abundance of salt over the fish could change the bottom line for the merchant or the fishermen. Time and time again, no matter how much care they took in preparing the salted fish, it always weighed in as West-Indies grade. Uncle Price fully understood Michael's frustration but also knew his limited options. He looked out to the sea and said, "Then what would we do if there was no merchant to take our salt fish, Mic?" Michael dropped his hands between his legs and replied, "It's just not right… The fish finally came in after all the years of catch'n nut'n and now we can't get the money for it… It's just not right…" Uncle Price looked at Michael Morgan and replied, "Right or wrong, there's nowhere else to go." He looked back at the sea with the black clouds forming on the dark horizon and continued, "If you keep flap'n yer gums, ya will never get that fish done, if that storm comes in." Michael Morgan looked toward the sea and replied with a nod, "I'd rather take that wind storm than the shit storm we'll get when we go to sell our fish to Dan Ryan…"

The fall fishery came in with good weather and a bad change of fishing fortunes for the Slate Harbour fishermen. While the spring and summer fish stocks appeared to be abundant, the fall fishery proved to be dismal. Early in the season, the government fisheries department had indicted the influx of extra codfish had been a short-termed anomaly, but the local fishermen believed the abundance of fish was going to be long-term. In the absence of codfish, the fishermen were dead wrong, and the scientist's assumption had been one hundred percent correct. On a cool fall morning, the light snow landing on the frigid waters of Slate Harbour gave the ageless sign. It was that time to store away fishing gear and haul the planked boats upon the wooden slip for the coming winter. Like clockwork, the signs of what to do and when to do it came with the changing seasons. It was all moving in the normal process, except for the oddity of selling the salted codfish. For the first time in countless years, the fish was not sold fresh to the local fish plant operator. Under the circumstances of having the union strike in place, the salt fish would be bought and sold to the fish merchant as they previously done many years ago.

Two weeks on, and Michael Morgan finally began to load his fully cured salt fish aboard his half-ton pickup. It was a day he dreaded, and something he had put off until pressure from his wife Martha pushed him to deal with the ghost of greed. With a slam of the tailgate, Matthew looked at his father with a grin and said, "Well, that's it, Fadder… With this load, we'll finally get some money for the season." His father didn't smile or reply. Michael Morgan just lit up his smoke and looked down at the best-salted cod he had ever seen. It was white, clean, and dried to perfection. Matthew was eager for an excellent response, so he encouragingly said, "I'd say we'll get top dollar for that fish!" Still no response, so he tried harder, "Hey, Fadder b'y!" Michael Morgan took a long suck on his short camel cigarette and finally said, "Don't get yer hopes up, boy…"

"But… It's perfect, Fadder! And we spent so much time on getting it perfect!"

"Oh… I know it's the best salt fish you'll ever see, but that two-legged shark will take a savage bite right off our perfect profits… I know he will…"

They arrived at Sharp's Cove and found an old broken building down by a busted-up wharf. In its day, that wharf was a bustling center of enterprise, where fishermen found the only avenue to sell their salt fish product. In that pinnacle place of business, skiffs were unloaded with salt fish from local fishermen, who were eagerly looking for a decent price. Sadly, load after load, they were given the lowest pay with no mercy. However, the merchants received the full market price when they shipped it far and wide as top-grade fish. It was a game of deceit and deception, where hardworking fishermen were given false excuses by hard-nosed men to devalue their perfect product. In the end, the poor fishermen found themselves nowhere to go and without options to make money for food and other essentials.

Standing on a dilapidated wharf was an older man with a strong attitude. Michael Morgan knew by the slant of his stance that he was a man molded from merchants of the past. He rolled down his truck window and asked, "Is Mr. Ryan handy?" The older man walked toward the truck, glanced at his fishy load, and leaned in through the window. With his gasoline breath, he growled, "Who are ya?"

"Morgan, Michael Morgan from Slate Harbour. I called earlier about the salt fish we have to sell."

"Well, I don't know if Mr. Ryan would buy that junk…" Michael knew right way that the games had started. The old man had his finger pointing toward Morgan's load of fish with a frown on his face when Michael Morgan strongly suggested, "Why don't you get yer crusty old gob out of me fook'n window and go get yer boss…"

The old man was not amused or shaken by Michael Morgan's surly suggestion. Back in the day, he had seen many strong-willed fishermen come to the wharf full of piss and vinegar and leave with their tail between their legs. He knew that when Mr. Ryan had his way, there would be another feisty fisherman leaving like a spent caplin upon an empty beach. The old man stepped back, chuckled, and said, "I'll get da old man, and I'll tell him there's an arse-hole with a load of shit for sale…"

Dan Ryan appeared from the old building with a cigar hanging from his mouth and a scowl upon his face. He didn't delay the inevitable. He walked directly over to the back of the truck and pretended to look at the fish in disgust. Dan Ryan stared at Michael Morgan in the face and asked sharply, "What do you want from me?" Michael and Matthew Morgan stepped out from the truck, and Michael asked, "You buy salt fish, don't you?"

"That depends…"

"Depends?"

"If the quality is good, I'll consider it…"

Michael Morgan had heard about the past stories of cagey fish merchants who could spin the heads of fishermen with their iron-handed arrogance. He knew it would take all the courage he could muster to keep from getting pushed around by those cunning merchants. But when the time came to deal with them in person, Michael Morgan wasn't prepared for the overbearing presence of an experienced fish merchant. Michael lowered his tone, and with a crack in his confidence, he said, "My fish is the best…"

Dan Ryan picked up one of the salted fish and quickly threw it down. He shook the salt from his hands and said, "It's under-salted and not clean…" Michael Morgan was so taken aback that he stuttered, "Bu… But it was heavily salted and cleaned to perfection…" Dan Ryan began to walk away but quickly turned around and asked loudly, "DID YOU EVER SELL SALTED FISH BEFORE?"

"No, but…"

"BUT NOTHING! You don't know nothing about it, and that's why your fish is junk…"

"I don't believe a word you say…"

Before Michael Morgan knew what was happening, Dan Ryan rushed to the back of the truck, picked up a heavily-salted fish and placed it in front of Michael Morgan's face. He shouted:

"WHAT DO YOU THINK THIS IS?"

"Good fish," Michael replied sheepishly.

"YOU THINK THIS IS GOOD FISH!" Without notice, Dan Ryan pushed the heavily salted fish directly into Michael Morgan's face and rubbed as hard as he could, while asking with his teeth clenched, "Now can you see it?" When he removed it, he said, "Now you know… This fish stinks and is not worth nothing…"

Matthew Morgan stood in silence and watched the pieces of salt fish slide down his father's face. Like everyone else from Slate Harbour, he had always seen him as a respected man and a pillar of the community. But at that moment, under the bright rays of the sun, the image of his belittled father had cast a shadow of sadness. Matthew looked down upon the fish and asked softly, "What do we do now, Fadder?"

Michael Morgan wiped his face, looked at his son, and replied, "We have nowhere to go, Son… And that prick knows it…"

Dan Ryan produced a broken smile and began to walk away until Michael Morgan asked, "How much will you give us?"

Stopping in his footsteps, Dan Ryan didn't turn around. He just looked at the old man with the gasoline breath and growled, "Give him West-Indy prices and not one penny more…"

On the way home, the sound of humming tires soothed the ringing of Dan Ryan's words that echoed in Michael Morgan's mind. With the smell of salt fish on his face and stink of money hanging in the air, Michael leaned in and switched on the radio. From the old dash speaker, the news broke the silence with a useless report. The fresh fish union strike was finally over with a loss of one cent per pound. It was a bitter price cut for the Morgan men and came too late to erase a smeared memory that went too deep. Michael turned off the radio and said with fragile confidence, "With fish so scarce, we'll have to come up with a different plan for next year, Son…"

Matthew knew his father had been humiliated by a reoccurring story that had happened time and time again to fishermen in the past. He had heard the stories of men who were left with only bread and molasses after bartering with greedy fish merchants like Dan Ryan. He may not have lived back in that day, but he fully understood the position those poor fishermen had been in. Matthew Morgan knew, with a cold winter coming without supplies, a real man would sacrifice his own pride to the ghosts of greed to keep his family fed. Matthew Morgan never mentioned the incident at Sharp's Cove on that day or any other day after. Over the sound of humming tires, he just looked at his father with a wide grin and said, "Next year will be better, Fadder…"

Chapter 7
Wolf on the Bank

Winter came and went, with long cold days and plenty of lean times for the Morgan family. The meager pay they received in the fall for their perfect salt fish provided little opportunity for extra supplies that winter. Each drop of heating oil was spread thin, and every ounce of food was stretched to the limit. The strain from the union strike and the stress from limited salt fish earnings had cracked their spirit but opened Michael Morgan's mind with the urgency for new possibilities.

At the kitchen window, Michael stared out at the melting ice and mumbled out loud, "If the fish are not on the grounds this season, I have another plan in me back pocket..." Martha poured light-colored tea halfway into his empty cup and replied, "Well, at least there'll be a fresh fish market, and you won't have to sell salt fish to that bugger, Dan Ryan..."

"It doesn't matter..." He took a loud sip of tea and continued, "No good of having a place to sell fish, with no fook'n fish to sell..." She put the kettle down and sat beside her husband. She sighed softly and said, "I can only cut baloney so thin, Mic..." Martha Morgan placed her wrinkled palms over his rough hands, and with a desperate tone, she continued, "You have to get fish…" They both looked out through the heavy-painted window with her hanging words, and she softly added, "We can't give up, Mic…" Michael Morgan took her soft hand in his, gave her a hard smile with a slow wink, and replied, "Nooo… We'll never give up…" He stared down upon the Morgan's Pride floating in the harbor and continued, "I have a plan…" Just as expected, the cod fishery started the way it had ended in the fall. On the fishing grounds outside Slate Harbour, fish were few on hooks and far between every net. Day after day the fishermen came to the wharf with empty fish holds and returned the next morning to try similar fishing methods in the same waters. After a time of this continual routine of trying the same fishing method in the same waters, Michael Morgan set his sights on trying the same fishing method in different waters.

The unusual activity aboard the Morgan's Pride wasn't overlooked by Uncle Price. Sitting on the wharf's edge, the excess number of items loaded aboard Michael Morgan's boat didn't add up for Uncle Price.

"What are ya load'n on board, Mic?"

"Oh, just the regular shit, Uncle Price…"

"Well, the Morgan's Pride seems to be carrying more shit today than yesterday…"

Uncle Price wasn't Michael Morgan's uncle. It was an endearing way by the folks in Slate Harbour to show respect for older men who lived in their community. But even though Price wasn't his uncle, Michael Morgan felt he was kin and knew he could trust him with anything. Michael laid down his filleting knife, climbed up on the wharf alongside

Uncle Price, and confided, "I'm going to try a new fishing ground out further, Uncle Price… Somewhere you may know."

"Well, I know just about all the fishing banks out there, and I also know they're a long way from the safety of Slate Harbour."

"With fish so scarce around here, I think it's time to take a chance or shit in me pants, Uncle Price."

"If I was a young man, I'd take me chance with you too, Mic…"

"I know you'd work circles around us young bastards back in the day, Uncle Price, but there is something you can do for me now…"

"Anything Mic…"

"Keep yer gob shut about this… There's only enough room on that small shoal for one boat."

"Now ya got me curious, Mic…"

"And you're not the only one… If Sam Black knows where I'm go'n, he'll be out there steal'n from my nets again…"

"But Mic, Sam Black hasn't made a peep since Buck O'Reilly beat him black and blue."

"That's because of the union strike last year… He was like everyone else… He was too busy fight'n with the salt fish merchants…"

"What makes ya think he'll go back to his old ways, Mic?"

Michael Morgan jumped down onto the deck of the Morgan's Pride, looked up at Uncle Price with a filleting knife in his hand, and answered, "Because he's a wounded dog, and that mangy bastard is more dangerous now than ever before..." He shook the filleting knife at Uncle Price with a grin and said, "Remember... Not a word to anybody..." Uncle Price smiled back at his good friend, placed a finger to his lips, and whispered, "Ya got yer uncle's word..."

Uncle Price's keen eye had seen extra supplies aboard the Morgan's Pride, and he knew Michael Morgan didn't intend on staying inshore. The tall pile of nets and rope reminded him of schooners in the past that would leave Slate Harbour with full decks of fishing supplies. Back then he was only a boy, but he remembered how they loaded the mounds of gear and sacks of grub to last a full trip, way out on the distant banks. Heading up from the wharf, Uncle Price had a good feeling about Michael Morgan's secret plan. He knew it was time something different had to be done and knew Michael Morgan was the man to do it. With satisfaction in every step, he bounded up the road and banged into somebody else, who also had seen unusual activity down aboard the Morgan's Pride.

Sam Black stepped into the path of Uncle Price and barked, "What's on da go, old man?" Uncle Price wasn't a fool and certainly not a friend of Sam Black. He stopped, hauled out the pipe hanging from his pocket, and lit it up. With a puff of thick smoke, he answered, "Nut'n."

"Seems more than nut'n get'n loaded aboard Morgan's boat..."

Another puff of smoke, and a similar answer from Uncle Price, "Nut'n more than usual to me..."

"Now lookie here, ya pile of wrinkly shit, you know something's on da go with that prick..." With an obvious fake facade, Sam pretended to ask, "Why don't ya spill yer guts to Uncle Sam?"

Uncle Price was aware Sam Black wanted to push his buttons and make him blurt out all the details. With another puff on the pipe, he looked at Sam Black with fake sincerity and said, "Well, b'y... I figure... most of his nets were damaged in that strange stage fire he had. He had too many holes in 'em, b'y... He's just put'n aboard more nets to make up the same net coverage... It just makes sense to me... Now, if ya can step out of me way, I'll be on me way..." Sam Black reluctantly stepped aside to let Uncle Price walk on. He took a few steps away from Black, knocked his pipe on a nearby post, and said, "I see yer scars are heal'n well, Sam..." Sam Black watched the back of old Uncle Price's head shake with suppressed laughter, and then asked calmly, "You know that old pipe ya have?"

"What about it?"

"Shove it up yer fook'n arse..." Nothing more was said or expected from Sam Black. Uncle Price removed the pipe from his front pocket and continued his way with confidence, that ships weren't sunk and no words were spoken from his loose lips.

High overhead, on board the Morgan's Pride, Matthew had seen the frosty exchange between Uncle Price and Sam Black. He had also heard the secret conversation between his father and Uncle Price. On the steel super-structure, high above the deck, Matthew Morgan placed himself in a precarious place, with the knowledge of what he had heard and seen from his lofty position. He quickly climbed down from the crow's nest and approached his father for answers.

"Fadder, when were you go'n tell me about your new plan?"

"Now."

"Where are we go'n, Fadder?"

"10 miles out, east by southeast…"

"But that's 10 miles straight out, Fadder…"

"Yes, and straight into the breeder fish."

"What's this place called, Fadder?"

Michael Morgan looked to the left and right, and said, "Wolf Owl Bank…"

"Wolf Owl?"

"Shush… Come in the wheelhouse, and I'll explain…"

Michael Morgan reached up and hauled out a tightly-rolled nautical chart and scurried down below to galley. Under the dim light over the galley table, he unrolled the chart and pointed down at a small shoal 10 nautical miles, east by southeast from Slate Harbour. Matthew looked briefly at the chart and said, "That's a strange name for a fishing bank…"

"Wipe da shit out of yer eyes, Son, and take another look…" Matthew leaned in over the chart and focused upon the point under his father's finger. He followed the contours of the shoal, and then the image popped right before his eyes.

"The shoal is in the shape of an owl!"

"Yes, b'y… Now ya can see where we're headed…"

"But, Fadder, where does the wolf come from?"

"Well, that's the strange thing about that special fishing ground…" He rolled up the chart and headed up to the wheelhouse with Matthew on his heels close behind. With the chart placed carefully upon control panel, he continued,

"If you don't get codfish there, you get wolf fish, and if you get the codfish, you won't see the face of an ugly wolf fish."

"Why's that, Fadder?"

"Maybe they can't stand each other… I don't fook'n know… All I know is we got a 50/50 chance to strike plenty of cod." Michael Morgan opened the wheelhouse door, and before he walked out, Matthew said, "And we got a 50 percent chance of get'n plenty of wolf fish too…"

"Yes, and you better keep an eye out for yer fingers, Son…"

"Why's that, Fadder?"

"'Cause those fishy wolf bastards are known for chomp'n the finger right clean off…"

The slamming of the wheelhouse door left Matthew Morgan alone with the smell of desperation from an empty fish hold. He watched his father step smartly on the deck through the wheelhouse window of the Morgan's Pride and then glanced toward the chart placed upon the control panel. With a slight smile on his lips and a proud look toward the deck, young Matthew Morgan embraced the newfound course for the Morgan's Pride with his father's new fiery spirit.

The next day, there was no sign of the Morgan's Pride in the light of day. Finally, under the cover of darkness, it slipped through Slate Harbour's narrow passage and docked in the shadow of the fish plant. Under the cloak of darkness, the Morgans had struck the motherload of codfish, but at midnight, with other fishermen fast asleep, the only ones there to witness the full load were the weigh master and Uncle Price.

"Holy shit, Mic! Ya got er stuffed to da gunwales!"

Soaked in his slippery oilskins, Michael Morgan looked up from the overflowing fish hold and said modestly, "She's not bad, Uncle Price..." Uncle Price slapped his knee and bellowed, "Not bad! Yer almost sunk, old man!" Quickly, Michael Morgan climbed upon the wharf and said with a stern tone, "You can't let this get out... I know it will get out in time, but we need a few days before to get the main body of fish. If the word gets out too soon, we'll be swamped with surrounding nets..." Uncle Price took a step back, did a quick tilt of his head, and hauled out the pipe from his pocket. Under the light of the moon, he took a quick inhale and said, "Listen here, Mic, I told you nobody would hear it from my lips, and I meant it..."

"Sorry, Uncle Price, I know you wouldn't leak it out... I'm a bit edgy, that's all..."

He took a quick puff and replied, "Don't worry, Mic, it's all good with me..." Without a warning, Uncle Price turned his back on Michael and started to climb down aboard the Morgan's Pride to join Matthew.

"Where the fook are you go'n, Uncle Price?"

"Somebody got to help you with this, or you'll never get it unloaded tonight..."

Michael Morgan turned to the weigh master and gave his brother-in-law a slow wink of understanding. After receiving a slow nod of disclosure in return, he joined his crew, and they began to unload the Morgan's Pride with wide grins under the full moon.

The tides of the week rose and fell, with empty boats for most and full loads for the Morgan's Pride. It was load and go in the dark early morning, and hoist and go in the dark late night. There was no time for breaks or boredom on board the Morgan's Pride as they hauled in the biggest kind of cod day after day. For a full week, their successful secret comings and goings were shut out from everyone until Friday night came, and then somebody opened their loose lips. With too much beer for weigh master to handle, Michael Morgan's brother-in-law had spilled every detail over the Slippery Squid bar.

Keeping good catches secret was a normal thing to do in Slate Harbour and every other harbor in Newfoundland. It was quite acceptable back in those days to keep the good fishing spots at close quarters and away from fellow fishermen. It was a normal practice and accepted by all fishermen as friendly competition in competitive times. With the exception of one, the fishermen at the Slippery Squid pub applauded the news about the secret strike of fish aboard the Morgan's Pride.

Outside the ring of friendly fishermen, Sam Black had been sitting in the corner of the bar in sullen silence when the groundbreaking news slipped out from the weighmaster. He just had been given permission to return to the Slippery Squid, and this was a bonus he didn't expect. In the shadow of the dim lit bar, Sam Black sipped his beer slowly, knowing that he needed more information to put him back into the spotlight of the Slippery Squid.

Saturday morning came with a pounding headache for Sam Black and a load of questions for his son, Junior. In the throbbing light of day, Sam Black cornered his son and said, "Go down on the wharf and find out what's going on with that arsehole Morgan…"

"Are you asking me to spy on him?"

"No. I'm telling you to spy on him…"

"What am I look'n for?"

"Any sign of where they got the fish…"

"I don't know about this…"

"Well, I do… Now get yer arse down on that wharf and start fish'n for details!"

Michael Morgan didn't take long to notice young Junior Black sneaking up the wharf. He was on full alert when Junior sat down on the wharf and began staring down onto the deck of the Morgan's Pride. In a flash, Michael Morgan stepped in front of his view and growled, "What da fook do you want?"

"Just look'n for Matthew, that's all…"

"Well, ya won't find him here…" Finding Junior hesitant to move on, Michael Morgan climbed upon the wharf ladder, stared him in the face, and said, "Why don't ya fly da fook back to coo coo's nest with that bird-brain fadder of yours?" There were no further questions needed. Junior stood up and walked on with his head hung down. With no answers and nothing to report, it seemed to be looking dim for Junior until his friend Matthew Morgan came strolling toward him in broad daylight.

"What's up, b'y…"

"Nut'n much, just head'n back to the boat before Fadder chews my head off…"

With a quick chuckle, they went on to have a brief conversation that only lasted a short time until they were spotted. High in crow's nest of the Morgan's Pride, Michael Morgan roared from the rigging at the top of his lungs, "MATTHEW! GET DA FOOK AWAY FROM HIM!" The message was clearly sent and quickly received with the abrupt parting of the young men and their curtailed conversation.

In short, Junior was standing in front of his impatient father with an absent look and an empty stomach. "Well, boy… What's on the go?" Junior watched his mother stir the steaming stew pot and replied, "No… I didn't hear anything about where they were going…"

"They had to fook'n say something!"

"No… Nut'n…"

The young man's grumbling stomach said it all. Lucy Black dished out a plate of hot stew and placed it on the table in front of her son. She knew he was only interested in food and there was nothing her husband could do but sit in silence and digest his half-eaten meal. While Lucy poured out the tea, young Junior spooned in the stew, and then blurted out with a belch, "All Matthew quickly said… Was… He was pissed off… It took two hours before they had breakfast on the grounds…" Sam Black slowly laid his cup down and asked inquisitively, "So… They had their breakfast just as they got to the grounds?" Junior didn't miss a beat with his fork. He took a hard swallow of stew and replied, "No… He said they took an hour to set the nets and then had breakfast." Sam Black wasn't a smart man, but he could subtract one from two, and that was more than he had before Lucy served up the stew. Just as he finished his brilliant calculation, young Junior looked at his father and said, "This stew is better than those fook'n wolf fish they're get'n too…" Lucy was quick to say, "Watch your language at the table, young man…"

Sam Black didn't care about the tone of language, but he did care about the topic of wolf fish being laid upon the table. He slowly took a sip of tea and asked, "What's this about wolf fish?"

"Matthew said they would get plenty of those ugly bastards when the nets went too far off the shoal areas."

"He did… did he?"

All the information was delivered at the table on a platter by Junior Black. He had provided all the information his father needed, without knowing he had filled in all the necessary blanks to the missing puzzle. Sam Black stood up from the table and went to the cabinet and hauled out a tightly rolled nautical chart. Unrolling it upon the table, he studied the distance. He said, "It would take them an hour from the harbor to get to…" Then put his finger down upon the shape of an owl. He looked up from chart and continued, "I need another job from you, Junior…"

"And what's that, Fadder?"

"I want you and yer buddy Matthew Morgan to go drink'n tomorrow night…"

"Whaaaaa?"

"I want you to get Matthew Morgan pie-eyed drunk tomorrow night."

"But…"

"No buts about it… I'll give you some money to get the job done…"

"But why?"

"Just do what yer told and shut yer mouth…"

Junior didn't ask any further questions and didn't care about his father's foolish questions. He was only too glad to drink free beer on his father's dime with Matthew Morgan.

Chapter 8
Bad Blood Rises

On the day of Junior's big drunk with Matthew Morgan, Sam Black needed his son's help with a different task. Moving meticulously over his gear in the morning, Sam Black shouted, "You pump the hydraulic oil and fill er' to the top."

"But why all the extra oil, Fadder?" His father tightened the turnbuckles and responded, "When you get that done, check the forward stays for wear."

"But we never checked the stays before, Fadder…" Without acknowledging his son, he said, "I'll check the engine oil…" Junior finished his task at the bow of the boat, stepped in front of his father in the engine room, and asked, "Why all the extra work, Fadder?" His father stared beyond the young man and said, "All I need now is you to put the grub aboard, and I'm all set…"

"Where are we headed, Fadder?"

"You're headed to the Slippery Squid tonight, and that's the only place you have to worry about…"

"That won't stop me from going in the morning!"

"You're go'n nowhere, boy…"

"What's all this about, Fadder?"

"This is about the job you have to do tonight... It's about get'n young Matty Morgan drunk and delaying that old prick from heading out to sea..."

"They're get'n so many fish, Fadder! Nut'n will stop them from going in the morn'n..."

"If you do your job, that young bastard will be go'n nowhere. He'll be blow'n bubbles in the bed when you get finished fill'n his gob with beer..." Sam Black slowly handed his son a fifty-dollar bill with a tight grip and received no further questions. His father reluctantly let go the money, leaned in close, and warned, "Don't fook it up, boy..."

It had been a long, hard week for the Morgan men. Every day involved a lengthy trip to and from the fishing grounds in all sorts of sea states. While on the fishing grounds, the continual hauling and heaving on nets never stopped until they were back to the plant with full loads. The steady process of hoisting bag after bag and weighing pound after pound wore the two Morgan men to the point where they were eager to see the end of a long week. With a heavy sigh of relief, Matthew turned off the wash-down hose and looked at his father.

"Well, that's it for this week."

"Yes, Son, we'll relax at home for tonight, and we'll be back at it again on tomorrow..."

"Tomorrow?"

"Yes, the plant extended its hours and will be open until our bunker loads are done." Matthew flicked the hose on the deck and said, "You can relax at home... I'm heading over to the Slippery Squid to have a few beers with Junior Black."

Michael Morgan knew better than to argue with a young man who needed to blow off steam in the company of his friends. He had been in the same situation when he was a young man and knew it wasn't a time to be a skipper or an enemy. Michael Morgan picked up the dribbling hose and said encouragingly, "We have an early start tomorrow, Son… Keep an eye on the time and try not to drink too much…" His father turned off the hose and realized his son would be with Junior Black. Without sounding too harsh, he said, "And remember… Don't say anything about where we're getting the fish, Son…"

"I won't say nut'n, Fadder…"

"You'll be in shark-infested waters with those Blacks…"

Matthew bounced off the boat and sprung it to the top of the wharf with rejuvenated energy. At that moment, he didn't care about sharks or the black waters he was about to enter. He shrugged off his father's shadowed warnings and shouted, "I'll be there on time… Like every other day…"

Later, at the Slippery Squid, the first beer slipped down easily for young Matthew Morgan. He had put in a hard week's work, and now he was finally in a place that didn't smell of slippery codfish or angry wolf fish. Downing the last drop of cold beer, Matthew was taken off guard with a hard smack on his back. Coughing, he shouted, "What da fook are ya at, Junior?"

"Suck it in, Morgan! The night is young, and there's plenty more cold beer…"

"I got to take it easy, Junior, I'm going fish'n in the morn'n."

"On Sunday?"

"I know… It's crazy, but the plant is opening up to take in the extra fish we're getting."

"Well, no need to worry about that now…" Junior got the bartender's eye with his fifty-dollar bill and said, "I'll have four beers, Reggie!"

"And now we're drinking two at a time, Junior?" Junior pushed the two beer toward Matthew, raised his bottle in the air, and gave a toast, "Fish on every hook… Two on some…" Matthew clinked his glass and gulped the beer down. Wiping his mouth, he exclaimed, "Now that's honeysuckle sweet, my friend…"

"Yes, b'y… You deserve a good night, and with this fifty-dollar bill, I'll make sure of it…"

Junior didn't like his father's despicable plan of delaying the Morgan's departure to the fishing ground, but he did enjoy Matthew's company at the Slippery Squid. For Junior, it was a roundabout way to spend some time drinking beer with a friend on his father's dime. It wasn't perfect, but it was better than being home under the boot of his burly father.

Beer after beer, they bailed them down, while everyone else in the Slippery Squid had come and gone. Looking up at the ship's clock that hung over the bar, the bartender squawked, "Time to get yer fook'n arses out of here, b'ys!"

"Just one more round, Reggie!"

"I'll tell ya what'll do for you sling-shits… I'll sell a couple of beers to go… And then ya can fly to fook home…"

Junior quickly grabbed the beer, threw the money on the bar, and left Reggie with the image of his middle finger. He slipped out the door with pie-eyed Matthew Morgan who stammered, "I, I, got to go home, b'y… I'm fish'n in da morn'n…"

"Don't worry, Matty, you'll be fine… Let's go across the road and sit on the church steps."

"But Father McCabe won't like it…"

"Fook 'em, Matty… That holy lump of shit don't like anything. Let's sit down here and have one more beer."

In his dark bedroom that overlooked the church steps, Father McCabe was having a restless night of tossing and turning. It was warmer than usual, and the priest had his window cracked, and his ears pealed for any stray sins that needed cleansing. On that warm night, the sound of two familiar voices through his opened window made him recall a confessional sin that he didn't want to remember.

Pointing toward Father McCabe's house, Junior laughed and sputtered, "I bet that old fook would flip his tunic for that hottie at the bar tonight… Hey, Matty?"

"Yes, b'y… She was something else… And those long legs… They were as high as Sharp's Point…"

"Ya… She'd send him run'n for da fook'n confessional box for sure…"

After a strong belly laugh and some clinking of beer bottles, the young men soon went silent over the church steps. In silence, they sipped their beer while Father McCabe stared upon the stark walls of his small room. Out of nowhere, with the buzz of the beer sinking in, Matthew's loose lips slipped upon the consecrated steps.

"Do, do, you know that my fadder had a fling with your mother?"

The sound of Junior swallowing his beer echoed off the church steps and into Father McCabe's opened window.

The priest silently lifted from his bed and blessed himself with holy water while he strained his thirsty ears.

On a night when sobering secrets were placed on sacred steps, Matthew Morgan and Father McCabe had expected a violent response from a drunken man. At the end of a long pause, Junior finished his beer with one swallow and then smashed the bottle upon the concrete steps. He stammered, "No... no wonder those fookers are at each other's throats..." Then he stood up from the steps, and slurred, "Come on, Morgan... Let's get da fook out of here... This place is creap'n me out..."

Alone in bed, Father McCabe looked up at the ceiling and wondered if the whole story would be told. In the darkness of the night, he prayed that the full impact of Lucy Black's confession would not be revealed by the lips of a drunken young man who had no idea of the implications it would cause. The priest quickly calmed himself and closed his eyes when he realized only he, Lucy, and God really knew the whole story.

Down by the water, the two young men perched upon the wharf in front of the Morgan's Pride. As they sat in silence, Junior threw a rock into the water and slurred, "Me... me and you are alike in many ways, Matt..."

"I... I... know... It's strange how our fadders are so different and we're so alike..."

"Well... Maybe those two are not so different..."

Drunken Matthew Morgan looked at two Junior Blacks who appeared to be floating from wharf to wharf and stammered, "Whaaa... What do... do... you mean, b'y..."

"Well, apparently they like the same women, don't they?"

"It… It… was only a fling, b'y, as far as I know…"

"What else do you know, Morgan?"

In his drunken state of dumbness, Matthew Morgan wavered back and forth upon the wharf and slurred, "All… All I know is… Da fook'n tide came in and da fook'n tide went out…"

"What da fook does that mean, Morgan?"

Matthew Morgan didn't know what exactly his father had meant with the rising and lowering of the tide, but he did know he shouldn't have told his drunken friend. Junior may have been filled to the gills with beer and staggering from pillar to post, but he understood the tide had washed in more than a simple fling. Junior grabbed Matthew's arm forcefully. "I said… What da fook does that mean?"

With Junior standing in between the rocks of the beach and no way out from the wharf, Matthew gave him the only thing he had left inside. He answered Junior by turning toward the water and throwing up his stomach into the rising tide. Junior held Matthew's arm tightly, knowing Matthew could accidently fall into the spinning tide without ever revealing the depth of his mother's tidal fling.

While waiting for answers that would never come from the intoxicated Matthew Morgan, Junior noticed a small light upon the horizon. Under the cover of a dark night, Junior Black saw a mast light that became dimmer as it moved east by south east from the mouth of Slate Harbour. At two in the morning, Junior knew the only fishing boat leaving at that hour would be the Morgan's Pride. With a tight grip on Matthew, who had left everything he knew floating on the water, he figured it would be strange for Michael Morgan to leave without his son. In a split second, with a quick head shift to right, Junior realized who had left in the dark. On the northside wharf, furthest out from them, the familiar empty space told him exactly whose light was becoming dimmer and whose father had left him on solid ground.

Michael Morgan didn't see the light leaving the Harbour while he stood in the kitchen and watched the kettle boil. Impatiently waiting for a son to emerge from his booze-smelling bedroom, he wasn't expecting anything different with the sea state on that morning. It was a just another morning, sipping on tea and stirring up past memories of times when he was a young man in wild waters. Michael Morgan desperately wanted to be at sea, but he knew it would be better to stand down this one time and give his son a wide berth of understanding. After a long week of hauling nets and pulling ropes, he thought it cruel to pull his son out of bed and into the cool morning for a long trip out to Wolf Owl Bank. For one exception of the week, he would take a walk down to the boat and wait there for an extra hour while his son slept and gathered his strength.

For Michael Morgan, it had the promise of a great morning with every step he took toward the Morgan's Pride. In the still morning air, with not a ripple on the water or a cloud in the moonlit sky, it was the best scenario for a perfect fishing trip. With no problems in sight, Michael stopped at the wharf's edge and noticed something strange on the distant horizon. Without warning, a voice from the corner of a shed said, "Mic, ya better take a look toward the northside of da harbor…"

"Uncle Price?"

"Yes, b'y…"

"What's up?"

"I couldn't sleep last night, and when I looked out the window, I noticed a boat heading out to sea… I knew it wasn't yours… Who was it?"

"Look toward the northside…"

Michael Morgan saw the empty berth where Sam Black's boat used to be and growled, "That bastard…"

"I guess he got information somewhere…"

Michael Morgan quickly realized, from Uncle Price's blunt remark, the perfect timing of Sam Black's departure and their untimely delay was not a fluke. He knew right away that his son had been fooled by a small fish, sent by a large shark with a thirst for trouble. Knowing the drunken state of his son, Michael Morgan asked, "By any chance, did you see if he was alone?"

"I came down to take a look, and only saw Sam in the wheelhouse…"

"That figures… The boy had done his job and was too drunk to go with him…"

"What are ya go'na do, Mic?"

"First, I'm go'na make sure I'm right, then, if I am right, I'm go'n fishing for shark…"

After a quick sprint to Sam Black's house, he barged in the door to find Lucy Black sitting at the kitchen table. In the small community of Slate Harbour, it was customary for folks to come and go each other's houses without notice or without knocking. On that morning, with Michael Morgan standing in her kitchen, she simple asked, "Do you want a cup of tea, Mic?"

"No… I'm not here for tea… Is the boy in bed?"

"Yes, b'y… He was too drunk to go with his father…"

Michael Morgan went to the room at the end the hall and walked inside.

"Where's yer fadder headed?"

Lost in a sickening sleep, Junior Black didn't know who or what had woken him up. He stared toward the dark silhouette standing in the doorway and slurred, "Who da fook are you… And what da fook are you do'n in me bedroom?"

"You know who I am, and you know I'm look'n for answers…"

"Well, there are no answers here…"

Young Junior Black pulled the blanket over his head and, in his muffled voice, he shouted, "Who in da fook wants those ugly wolf fish anyway…"

Michael Morgan backed out of the room with clear answers. He knew exactly where Sam Black was headed and understood perfectly well what he had to do. In the kitchen, Lucy knew about the strong dangerous current that flowed between her husband and her previous lover. She stopped Michael at the door and said, "I know he does some stupid things, but he's a good man sometimes too…"

"Good men don't steal from other men's nets, Lucy…"

"I know he's out of control, Mic, but why don't you leave it be?"

"Too late for that…"

"What are you going to do?"

From the doorway, Michael Morgan left Lucy with, "If I catch him haul'n my nets today, he may find himself with more than a dangerous bite from an ugly wolf fish…" Knowing her husband was in peril on sea, Lucy quickly called the one person who had never let her down in times of trouble.

Michael Morgan boarded the Morgan's Pride to find his son waiting in the wheelhouse. In his mind, there was no sense getting mad with a son who couldn't fathom the depth of deception by a fake friend. He just said, "You're too sick to be going this morn'n, Son…"

"I'll be alright, Fadder… I'll sober up on the way out to the fishing grounds…" Michael Morgan didn't want his son on board a boat headed for stormy seas and didn't mind saying it. "Take yer sick arse home, Son… I don't need you today…"

"But you'll be alone on the bank…"

"Oh… I got a feel'n I won't be alone…"

Too green around the gills to grasp his father's words, the young man staggered his way off the boat and toward their home that overlooked the harbor.

Out of sight from his son, Michael Morgan went to his truck and took a shotgun from behind the seat. In an angry trance, he placed the gun tightly by his side and began to walk out the wharf until he was stopped by a familiar voice.

"Are you going to shoot some birds while out fish'n, Mic?"

Michael Morgan looked toward the open sky and replied, "Yes, Father McCabe… That's exactly what I had in mind…"

"A bit early in the fall, Mic, for shoot'n birds, though, Mic…"

"Maybe I'll get lucky and catch one in the act…"

Father McCabe stepped in front of Michael Morgan, stared at the gun tucked closely by his side, and said, "Mic… Lucy called and told me what's going on…"

"You don't understand, Fadder John… That man is gone out to steal my fish…"

"Mic, you don't understand… There's more to this than you think…" Michael Morgan stepped closer to the priest and asked, "What is it that I don't know, Father McCabe?"

Father McCabe's faith was strong, and his commitment to the holy order was even stronger. Words whispered in the sacred confessional box were not his to say. He couldn't breach his vow of silence, even if the hidden truth could stop a man from committing a mortal sin. In a moment when the religious duty was balanced with truth, Father McCabe chose selected silence.

"Mic, you're a good man… I'll leave it in the hands of God that you'll do the right thing."

"Untie my bowline, Fadder John… If Sam Black is mess'n with my nets, I'm sure I'll do the right thing…" Michael white-knuckled the throttle lever and left Father McCabe standing on the wharf, soaking in his good intentions. In his hasty departure, Michael Morgan needed space from what he used to know and time to think about doing the right thing.

Chapter 9
Storm of Spite

As the minutes went by, Michael Morgan's tight grip upon the wooden wheel of Morgan's Pride slowly eased. In times of trouble, Father McCabe had always entered his mind when stormy thoughts could come from the rough waters of life. When Sam Black's antics would push his brain to the point of perilous reactions, it seemed his holy friend was always there to pull him back from the brink of barbed madness. As the waves lifted and lowered his body through the soothing sea, calmness returned to his mind and settled him down with Father McCabe's words of reasoning. Halfway to Wolf Owl Bank, Michael Morgan slackened the throttle lever to three-quarter speed and began to remember a time many years ago when he went too far with a troubled woman.

Back in a time when youth was beauty, there was no finer example than Lucy Black. She was young, full of life, and head over heels for a dangerous man who had no respect for women. Lucy had played with the fire and found herself time and time again, scorched by abusive behavior from a brute who treated her like a burnt offering. Michael Morgan had watched their stormy relationship from a solid shore of understanding while he waited to save her from the dark depths of Sam Black. He knew her volatile relationship would send her on a wave of emotional turmoil that would eventually have her crashing on the shore that he stood upon.

Michael Morgan squeezed the wooded wheel as he recalled the night when she came to him at the Slippery Squid bruised and beaten. He remembered her soft touch and searching eyes, seeking something from someone who could take her from stormy seas and lay her in calm waters. On a night when the tide of passion came in and out, a fleeting love was found in the safety of Michael Morgan's safe harbor. Michael Morgan released the wooded wheel and thought back on the morning after. He remembered vividly, Lucy throwing back the sheets and leaving him to head out into the red skies that hung over Sam Black.

In drunken state, Sam Black had mistreated his woman and didn't miss her from his tight grip until the morning after. What followed was a wave of suspicion that came and went, with Black's continual tide of anger. Michael Morgan was well-aware that Sam Black knew something had happened between him and Lucy, but he also knew Sam Black didn't know the depth to which the encounter had sunk. From that time on, Sam Black never forgave his woman for something he didn't know and never forgot a man for something he thought he knew.

With only a few minutes to go, the wind began to blow fresh across the opened deck of the Morgan's Pride. Under blueberry skies and over bright white-capped seas, his senses awakened and brought him back to reality. From a distance, he could see the boat with the broken mast through foaming spray. There it was in full form, floating over the sweetest shoal on Wolf Owl Bank.

Michael Morgan hauled back the throttle lever from three-quarter speed to half speed as he inched closer to his target with Father McCabe's words ringing in his mind. In this calmer state, on choppy waters, he could no longer see himself using a gun to send a message that could be done with a voice of reason. In his mind, he would lay down his arms and find the words to stop the flow of bad blood. Back to quarter speed, the boat with the broken jib was in clear view and dead straight ahead.

Everything changed when Sam Black was directly in his sights. The boat with the broken jib sent a shot of cold shivers down his back and a rush of hot blood to his brain. While the Morgan's Pride began to rock from side to side, Father McCabe's peaceful message faded away with the fresh sight of an old foe.

In the center of the boat, Sam Black was staring directly at him as he hauled the full net. Once again, Michael Morgan's blood began to boil when he put the binoculars to his eyes and confirmed the inevitable. There he was in perfect view, taking the fish from Michael Morgan's net. Laughing straight in his face, Sam Black gave a crystal-clear message. Michael Morgan's emotional wounds were rubbed raw by the smirk of satisfaction on Sam Black's smug face.

Blackness shaded his mind as he watched. In full view, with his midship facing the Morgan's pride, Sam Black proudly placed his middle finger squarely in the sights of Michael Morgan. In the wake of Sam's rebellious response and in the psychotic state of Michael Morgan's mind, the shotgun was no longer needed on deck. He white-knuckled the throttle lever to full speed and lined up the Morgan's Pride stem with Sam Black's raised middle finger.

The Morgan's Pride was unique, unlike many vessels in Slate Harbour. Michael Morgan had built the boat himself with a specific purpose in mind. In early spring, when the seal hunt started on the ice fields, he needed a boat that could withstand the pounding impact of the thick glacial ice. Only heavy, seasoned juniper lumber was selected and used to build the stem and the ribs of his boat. Every thick oak plank was fastened with stainless screws, drilled deep within the hardened juniper stem. It was built to last and built to blast through thick dark ice. Now, its hardened juniper stem and thick oak planks were headed for Sam Black midship at full speed.

Maybe Sam Black couldn't grasp the final moments when the juniper stem of the Morgan's Pride went beyond the point of no return. Perhaps, in the moment of getting caught by the person he hated most in life, his adrenalin accelerated to the point of intoxication. Maybe he just went mad. For whatever reason, Sam Black continued to stretch his middle finger, while he smiled at the white-waked boat approaching under full throttle. With his other hand behind his back and seconds to impact, Sam Black played his last defiant move with sharp intent to kill. While he continued to hold his middle finger in Michael Morgan's crosshairs, he hurled his homemade axe directly at the Morgan's Pride wheelhouse with his hidden hand.

Just before impact, Michael Morgan didn't hear the thud from the homemade axe that lodged between his two wheelhouse windows. In his psychotic state, he was on a delusional mission caused by the unrelenting acts of defiance committed by the deranged Sam Black. Aiming his strong stem toward Sam Black, he had lost complete touch with reality until he crashed into the midship of the boat with the broken jib.

The reinforced juniper stem of the Morgan's Pride sliced through Sam Black's midship like a fish prong stabbing the soft belly of a codfish. It hit hard, and it went deep. Pine plank splinters fired in all directions, and the boat with the broken jib split in smithereens. In the midst of the carnage, Sam Black bobbed for air amongst the tangle of ropes and planks. Gasping, he shouted, "I'll FOOK'N CUT YA, MORGAN!"

Out on the bow, with the fresh wind blowing hard against Michael Morgan's mind, he finally returned to reality and realized what he had done. He quickly made his way to the open deck, grabbed a heaving line, and threw it as hard as he could at Sam Black.

"GRAB ON, BLACK!"

Tangled up in rope and bleeding from lower extremities, Sam Black wanted no help from Michael Morgan. The sharp-edged winch-table had sliced him wide open, leaving his internal organs exposed to the whims of the Labrador current. Wallowing in a sea of his own blood, he would never accept help from Michael Morgan, even if he were the last person on the planet. He could see Michael Morgan fading in and out, knowing he wanted to save him after trying to kill him. Sam Black wanted no part of Michael

Morgan's heroic effort. From his blurred vision, he watched the man he most hated shout from the top of his lungs.

"GRAB THE ROPE, BLACK!"
"YOU'LL HANG FROM DA FOOK'N ROPE, MORGAN…"
"JUST TAKE THE GOD-DAMN ROPE!"

Sam Black searched and found the final solution to end his misery and pain. A large anchor had lodged on the stern of his boat from the impact of the Morgan's Pride. That anchor had been on the bow of the Morgan's Pride, but after the impact, it was an object in motion until it rested upon the stern of the boat with the broken jib. Sam realized the rope from the anchor had flung everywhere, including around his body. In the floating wreck, he reached and grabbed onto a long-handled gaff. With all his remaining might, he struck the teetering anchor on the stern of the boat. Michael Morgan cried out in vain, "DON'T, SAM… I'LL SAVE YA…"

White foam drooled down from Sam Black's scowl as he glanced at the fading face of Michael Morgan. With false energy, he growled, "YOU'LL SAVE ME IN HELL, YA FOOK'N BASTARD…"

Another smack from the gaff, aided by a large sea swell, finally did the job. The anchor slowly rocked for a second and then rolled over the stern. As the rope reeled out at full speed from the weight of the heavy anchor, Michael Morgan cried out, "I'M SORRY, SAM…" From the midship of a sinking wreck, Sam Black filled his lungs with air, and with his last breath, he cried out, "FOOK YOU, MORGAN..."

Right before Michael Morgan's eyes, the defiant Sam Black's body was flushed down into the cold deep ocean. He had succumbed to the frigid sea with the last bit of spite he could muster. Left on the surface of the sea was a broken jib and a damaged soul.

Besides the absent anchor and a few missing flakes of paint from the stem, the Morgan's Pride was not visibly damaged. The reinforced stem had held up well from the impact, and all the stainless screws were accounted for. Yes, the Morgan's Pride's physical damage was minimal, but the internal damage for its skipper was extensive. In one burst of madness, Michael Morgan quickly realized the salty taste of revenge would sting his soul for the rest of his life.

One by one, the larger remnants of the boat with the broken jib shattered and sunk below the surface, leaving only a small debris patch on a large ocean. In a short time later, there was very little left to see or find from the final encounter between Michael Morgan and Sam Black. The murder on Wolf Owl Bank would be lost to the tides of time and hidden from anyone who wondered what had happened to the boat with the broken jib and its surly skipper.

The trip home was difficult for Michael Morgan, knowing he had caused the death of Sam Black. He had always been a church-going man who believed in the philosophy of peace and the concept of love. Now, with the Morgan's Pride's blood-stained stem plowing through the increasing waves, he felt an empty space where his soul used to be. With every wave that crashed upon wheelhouse windows, his mind became detached from a sense of reality.

In his absent state of awareness, he didn't realize the wind had increased to storm force strength.

Michael Morgan was lost in a sea of regret when the VHF radio blasted, "MAY DAY…. MAY DAY… MAY DAY… THIS IS, THE SEA CHALLENGER… LATITUDE 52… LONGITUDE 30… OFF SHARP'S POINT… OUR HULL HAS BEEN BREACHED AND WE'RE SINKING FAST…"

Michael Morgan knew the area around Sharp's Point very well. It was well-known that over the years, countless boats had sunk when they struck the shoal rocks off Sharp's Point. Between the fishing banks and Slate Harbour, Sharp's Point was halfway to a safe harbor and in the middle of nowhere. Jutting out far from land, it was an extremely shoal point that would prove to be a nightmare time and time again for boats that were caught in the rage of unexpected wind.

When the call came, involuntary reaction took over his own feelings of deep remorse and fathomless regret. Hearing of a boat in distress on the water, Michael Morgan immediately blocked his mind and grabbed the VHF microphone. "This is the Morgan's Pride, Sea Challenger… Hang on, I'm on my way…"

The advancing storm moved in fast and furious, pushing the deadly incident on Wolf Owl Bank at the back of Michael Morgan's mind. There was no time to dwell on himself. He had a distress call blaring on the emergency channel that demanded his full attention. For now, his incendiary thoughts of disaster would be temporarily blocked until he dealt with his involuntary response of rescue.

From a distance, the remnants of Sea Challenger could be seen scattered all around the shoal rocks of Sharp's Point. In among the debris, Michael Morgan could clearly see the crew's bobbing heads in the frigid water. There was no time to think or delay. Plowing through shallow cresting waves, in between the countless rocks, Michael Morgan placed himself and the Morgan's Pride in harm's way at full speed. He knew full well that they had only minutes before the crew would succumb to the ocean's cold-water grasp.

As the beaming navigational lights of the Morgan's Pride became brighter and brighter, the soaked crew waved harder and harder. They couldn't believe their eyes to see the Morgan's Pride had arrived through the mountainous swell and wash of the cresting waves. Their savior had risked himself and his boat to reach them in the nick of time, in the white-water shoals.

Michael Morgan eased back on the throttle, and then slowly but surely, the Morgan's Pride soaked alongside the soggy men of the Sea Challenger. One by one, they were picked from the reluctant sea and settled down below in the galley of the Morgan's Pride. The skipper of the Sea Challenger was the last one to be hauled aboard and first one to refuse going down below.

Standing side by side with the skipper of the Morgan's Pride, soaked, Skipper James Ballard scanned over the remnants of his tattered boat in the rock-infested waters and said, "You're a brave skipper to take your boat in these dangerous waters… We owe you our lives…"

Most everyone knew each other in their area of Newfoundland, especially the skippers of fishing vessels. Michael Morgan knew of the Sea Challenger and was fully aware exactly who the skipper of the vessel was. "You would have done the same for me Jimmy..."

"Maybe so, Mic, but steaming through those shoals at full speed was a suicide mission..."

"Just trying to get to you men as fast as possible, that's all..."

Skipper James certainly appreciated being plucked from the icy water, but in all his years at sea, he never saw such a reckless act that ended so well. He was perplexed with Michael Morgan's daredevil move but pleased to see the smiling faces down below in the galley of the Morgan's Pride. For the crew, help had come just in time, and they didn't care at what speed or at what cost for the heroic skipper.

Back in Slate Harbour, the unexpected northeaster storm was not an unusual event. From time to time, an unpredictable wind would come from any point of the compass without warning.

In the past, many fishermen lost their lives at sea when wild winds came from nowhere and swept their boats from the surface. However, for the Sea Challenger, tragedy had been adverted by one brave but foolhardy skipper of the Morgan's Pride.

Quickly, the word had been spread around the surrounding communities until almost everyone knew what had happened at the height of the storm. For the family and friends of the Sea Challenger's crew, their prayers had been answered, but for others, the good word did not come. For those, the storm raged on without the knowledge of what happened to the boat with the broken jib.

Overlooking the harbor, from three different lookouts, eyes scanned the white water for a boat that couldn't come home. Waiting in vain was a son, a wife, and a priest who knew there had been more than one storm brewing that day. The lashing wind and pouring rain weren't the only force they feared. They all knew, with the bad wind blowing from a dark place, the chance of sighting the boat with the broken jib were very slim.

Junior Black had seen his father's stormy eyes and watched him leave toward a reoccurring task of retaliation. He never understood why his father had to push Michael Morgan so hard, but he did know that someday, the ramification could come under dark skies.

Lucy Black had seen her husband's fury many times. She knew his idea of communication came in the form of a clenched fist. She also had seen the rift between Sam and Michael grow deeper than the blackened sea that tossed before her tortured eyes.

Father McCabe had seen Sam Black apply his full pressure of provoking Michael Morgan on many occasions. He understood quite well that Sam Black's heavy words could push a peaceful man over the thin edge of patience. The priest also knew a secret from the confession box that could capsize a man's boat with a soft whisper.

All three knew there was a strong undercurrent of turbulent waters between both men. The possibility of a tidal wave of devastation played heavily on their minds as they stood and stared toward the angry sea. In the wild wind and the ragged rain, three sad souls waited in vain for the fate of another soul who had gone down in the undertow of revenge.

On the Slate Harbour wharf, people were standing on every plank, watching the Morgan's Pride as it entered the Harbour with the sound of car horns blaring out a hero's welcome. The Morgan's Pride proudly plowed through the narrow harbor opening and settled back into still protected waters. Even before they lashed the boat to the wharf, anxious onlookers boarded the Morgan's Pride to welcome home the survivors and their heroic savior.

The outpouring of joy could be seen above and below the deck of the Morgan's Pride. It seemed like everyone in Slate Harbour had come out to pour gratitude upon the skipper who had saved all aboard the Sea Challenger. Everyone, with the exception of a mother and son, were jumping for joy as they embraced the ones that were saved from the angry sea.

Standing on the wharf with prayers that couldn't be answered, Lucy and Junior Black had gone down to the wharf, where the boat with the broken jib used to be.

"Somethings wrong, Son… I can feel it inside…"

"He'll come home, Mudder… He's seen many rouge storms before…"

"Yes, he's seen many stormy seas… But the storm of revenge could lash out bigger trouble than an angry sea…"

"What do you mean, Mudder?"

"I'm just say'n… Yer fadder left in a storm of spite, and Michael Morgan left in a gale of revenge…"

"What are ya talk'n about, Mudder?"

Lucy Black took a long blank stare at her son without a reply until he prodded, "I need answers, Mudder…" Looking out over the foaming sea, she finally answered, "I got some questions of my own, Son…"

Chapter 10
Clouds of Concern

Father McCabe didn't join the joyous crowd that were schooled around Michael Morgan's battered boat. He was alone in the chapel, praying for a lost soul who hadn't found his way home. Many times in the past, he had seen a sudden northeastern gale come from nowhere to take fishermen down into the depths of the ocean. This was an unfortunate reality that came from making a living from the sea, and everyone who lived in their small fishing community fully understood that danger. On his knees, under the light of a dim candle, Father McCabe also understood this possibility, but this particular time, he wasn't worried about the wrath of the sea. This time he prayed that a different type of storm didn't lash out from the depths of darkness and send Sam Black to his final resting place.

In the chapel by the sea, Father McCabe remembered Michael Morgan's wild rant when he cast off from the wharf that morning. The priest cautiously lit another candle and didn't pray for the ones in peril by the sea. He bowed his head and deeply prayed for one man who may have had lost his way, and another who may have been lost to eternity. In silent prayer, Father McCabe heard the soft footsteps approaching from behind, and without raising his head, he said, "Have faith, Lucy… The storm will blow over, and Sam will make it home."

"I'm not worried about the storm, Father… And I don't think he's coming home…" The priest lifted his head and opened his eyes to ask, "Why do you think he's not coming home?"

"Michael Morgan was at the house this morning in a rage…"

"Their bows have crossed many times before, Lucy… Why would this be different?" "Michael had a look in his eyes that I have never seen, Father…"

"I see…"

"No… You have never seen that side of Michael Morgan…"

"He's a good man, Lucy…"

"Yes, Father, he's a good man, but good men can have dark sides too…"

"Maybe so…"

Both sat in the pew in front of the altar, and after some time, the priest said, "You should have told Sam a long time ago…"

"Then they would be looking for me for a long time…"

"I know he's been abusive, but he wouldn't have gone that far, my child."

"If Sam knew… he would have thrown me overboard without blink'n an eye."

"Then what about Michael? Shouldn't you have told him?"

"It would have been too complicated, and everyone would have suffered more."

"Then what about…"

"He'll never know…" With a strong searching look from the priest, she finished, "Ever…"

"Even if something happened to Sam?"

Lucy Black stood up and slowly lit another candle. She sat back down beside the priest and said, "Well, that could change everything… And I don't want to think about that tonight…" Father John McCabe never replied; he just looked over toward the confessional box and blessed himself very slowly. Knowing that he had been caught in a sea of deception and couldn't speak the truth without breaking a crucial vow of his priesthood, he was sinking deeper in secrecy. It was a silence that sliced at his very soul. He took Lucy Black's hand and said, "My child, this sea of deception is so big, and my boat of delusion is so small…"

"Pardon me, Father?"

The priest stood and said, "Don't forget to light another candle."

"For Sam or Michael?"

He grabbed his hat from the pew and replied, "For me…"

"Where are you headed, Father?"

"I'm going to welcome home a hero…"

"Yes… Michael Morgan saved all those from the sunken Sea Challenger."

As he opened the door, Father McCabe turned and left Lucy with, "I hope it's not too late to save the savior… Good night, Lucy."

Father McCabe could clearly see the Morgan's Pride from a distance. The boat was lit up like a church, with souls of all sorts hanging from below and above deck. It was very evident to the priest, by the sound of laughter and continual show of high fives, that smiles were not in short supply. But, as Father McCabe got to the wharf, he noticed in the center of the celebrations, there was a silhouette of a skipper with his head hung down.

The crowd parted tight to the bulkheads as Father McCabe approached Michael Morgan. Reaching out his hand, Father McCabe said, "You've saved the day for these men and their families… Well done." Shaking the priest's hand, without looking at him straight in the eyes, Michael Morgan replied, "Anyone would have done the same, Father John…"

"Maybe so, but you were tested, and you came through for those men."

"I just did the right thing…"

"Did you do the right thing for Sam Black, Michael?"

Father McCabe was a seasoned man of the cloth and knew how to read his parishioners well. He had seen them at their highest, when the light in their eyes shined out like beacons of hope. Father McCabe also had seen them at their lowest, where their sad faces told stories that cast long shadows. From the lack of eye contact and the tight ridge around Michael Morgan's face, Father McCabe suggested, "Let's go out on the wharf, Michael, and get some fresh air…"

Under the clear skies and diminishing winds, Father McCabe hoped his dark suspicion could provide light upon the missing boat with the broken jib. Michael began, "Father John, I know I took a chance at Sharp's Point, but those men were going to die…"

"Listen, Michael… I know you took a daring chance, but you saved their dear lives and that's what mattered… But I'm not worried about the chance you took with them… I'm worried about the chance you took with Sam Black…"

"What do you mean?"

"I saw you with that rifle this morning… And I heard from Lucy that you were in a rage with Sam Black… And we all know he hasn't returned…"

"It was a big storm out there today…"

"I'm not talking about the storm from the sea… I'm taking about the storm inside of you!" Michael Morgan didn't respond to Father McCabe's stormy accusation. In the darkness of the night, he sat under the shade of a broken light pole. Father McCabe sat on the opposite side of the pole without facing the man and then placed his scapular around his neck. He blessed himself and said, "Confess your sins, my son; they will not go beyond this holy ground."

With the rush of the ocean swell from the calming seas, Michael Morgan placed his head down and softly said, "Bless me, Father, for I have sinned…" After a pause from Michael, the priest encouraged, "Go on, my son…"

"Everything you told me about forgiveness was playing in my head on the way out to Wolf Owl Bank… I believed in turning the other cheek… I believed in starting over… I believed in putting it all behind us… And then Sam appeared from the mist… Everything went dark and cloudy… I couldn't think… All I could see was Sam's slimy grin and his middle finger in front of my face… I lost it…"

"What happened then, Michael?"

"I pushed throttle at full and struck him midship…"

"Did he survive the impact?"

"Yes, and I came to my senses and tried to throw him a lifeline."

"Did he take it?"

"No… He would never take help from me…"

"What happened then?"

"He was entangled in my anchor that was logged on his sinking wreckage…"

"And? What did he do?"

"He pushed the anchor into the sea with his gaff and said, fook you…"

With the moonbeam finding the truthful face of Michael Morgan, he finished, "He was flushed down with the anchor, and I never saw him again…" Father McCabe stood and went to the side of Michael and said, "You may have caused his death, but you didn't kill him…"

"What's the difference, Father… He's dead by my hand…"

"He's dead by the hands of both of you… And I believe the court will give you lenience in this case…"

"There won't be a case."

"But you have to report this, Michael…"

"No reporting from me… Or you…"

"But…."

"No…" He pointed down upon the ground they stood and stated, "You said this was holy ground… And what's said in the confessional is kept in the confessional…"

Under the weight of two confessional secrets, the burden of truth became too heavy for one priest to bear that night. He couldn't continue any further, knowing there was truth in keeping his vow of silence and a lie in keeping a secret that caused a mortal sin. Struggling for each step, Father John McCabe stumbled out the wharf without seeing young Junior Black waiting at the crest of the rocky shore.

Junior watched the priest rub his polished beads and bow his heavy head while he stood in the shadow of the wharf, leering at the Morgan's Pride. Just as Michael Morgan began to walk back toward the Morgan's Pride, Junior Black shouted from the shadow of the wharf, "MORGAN!" Michael backed away from the boat and headed toward the voice that came from a dark place. Knowing Michael Morgan expected him, Junior grunted, "Did you see fadder?"

"No... I'm sure he'll be alright... He may have anchored off in a sheltered bay."

"Didn't you see him on Wolf Owl Bank?"

"He must have gone to another fishing bank..."

"No... He was on Wolf Owl Bank..."

"How did you know he was headed there?"

"That don't matter..."

"Oh... I get it... You got Matt drunk... And he spilled his guts to you, then you delayed us leaving in the morn'n..."

"Nobody owns Wolf Owl Bank, Morgan..."

"We were there first! And your old man couldn't stand us get'n fish..."

"It's a free sea, and he had the right to go anywhere he wanted..."

"That's true... But he had no right to take fish from my nets..."

"On Wolf Owl Bank?"

"On any bank..."

"You saw him this morn'n, didn't you?"

"No."

"Did you scuttle fadder's boat?"

"No… Now fook off and leave me alone…"

Michael Morgan quickly turned and walked toward the Morgan's Pride, followed by Junior Black, who was catching up. They were walking briskly, heel for heel, until Junior Black stopped dead in his steps and shouted, "WHAT THE FOOK IS THAT?"

Back on Wolf Owl Bank, when Michael Morgan was lost in rage and headed for the boat with the broken jib, he never saw Sam Black's last act of defiance. He didn't realize Black tried to split him open like a salted codfish, just before he rammed the boat. He was unaware that the axe had found its mark between the two wheelhouse windows and out of his range of sight. But, under the light of the full moon, it was plain to see Sam Black's axe was lodged directly in the middle of the wheelhouse windows. Junior Black lunged towards Michael Morgan and demanded, "Where the fook is my fadder, Morgan…"

"I don't fook'n know, I told ya…"

Pointing toward the axe lodged between the wheelhouse windows, he exclaimed, "OH, you know! Now, where the fook is he?"

"He threw that axe at me this morning before he headed out."

"YOU'RE A LIAR!"

"You can believe me or not, but that's the truth!"

"The old man said you Morgans were all good-for-nut'n liars, and he was right!"

"Why don't you fly the fook out of here, Junior…"

Junior Black jumped upon the front of the Morgan's Pride, and with two hands, he dislodged the axe. He shook the axe and replied, "Not without take'n this evidence…"

Down at the Royal Canadian Mounted police station, they already heard about the missing man from Lucy Black. They relayed the information to the coastguard, and everything was in place to investigate at daylight. The Mounties appeared to have everything in order and all the necessary details needed to organize their search, until the son of the missing man entered the station door bearing new information.

"Yes, Junior…"

"I want to report a murder."

"Excuse me?"

"My fadder was murdered by Michael Morgan."

"Easy… Son… I know it's hard for you… But we'll find him at daylight."

"Well, you won't find him alive…"

"What makes you think he's not alive?"

In Slate Harbour, the atmosphere at the Royal Canadian Mounted police station had always been laid-back. Serving rural communities in the middle of nowhere, required no need to have pistols locked and loaded. It was a peaceful place where Mounties could work without fear of losing their lives to senseless violence. On that evening, just before their coffee and donuts were passed around, the tranquility of their peaceful world was shattered when Junior Black raised the concealed axe to show his evidence. Scrambling from their desks, the two Mounties approached the young man carefully. The senior Mountie gingerly said, "Eee-asy, Junior... We'll find your father... There's no need for violence... Just put the axe down..."

Junior placed the axe upon the station counter and said, "I removed this axe from the wheelhouse of the Morgan's Pride... And it was my father's axe..."

Quickly realizing it was placed on the counter for display purposes only, the Mountie gently took the axe into their possession and asked, "What does this axe have to do with your missing father?"

"Michael Morgan murdered him on Wolf Owl Bank."

"With this axe?"

"I don't know how he killed him. I just know he did..."

The two Mounties looked at each other, and the senior officer said, "I know it's hard to have your father missing, but there was an unexpected storm and sometimes, unfortunately, that's normal..."

"It wasn't a storm that took my Fadder... It was Michael Morgan..."

"Listen... We all know Michael Morgan and your father weren't exactly friends, but that doesn't mean they would kill each other. Furthermore, Michael Morgan is a pillar of the community! For God's sake... He even rescued all hands aboard the Sea Challenger!" The junior Mountie stepped in, adding, "He risked his own life and saved those drowning men! Does that sound like a man who would murder someone?" The senior Mountie placed his hand on Junior Black's shoulder and said, "I know you're distraught, but we'll find your father, Son. We have resources and the manpower to do it." Junior Black snapped his shoulder back from the Mountie's hand and sneered, "I'm not your son, now give me back my axe."

In a more serious tone, the senior Mountie said, "We'll hold the axe for now, Junior… Just in case someone gets hurt."

"It's too late for that… While you arseholes are here drink'n coffee, the evidence is drift'n with the tide."

"I think it's time for you to head home, Junior…"

The station door shut behind the angry man, leaving the two Mounties shaking their heads. The junior Mountie asked his supervisor, "What do you make of that, sir?"

"My grandfather from Grand Falls had a saying about guys like him."

"What was it, sir?"

"Water seeks its own source…"

"What does that mean, sir?"

"The boy is Sam Black's son… Need I say more?" With a slow shake of the head from the junior Mountie and a quick wink of the eye from the senior Mountie, the command was given, "Let's have coffee." Relaxing with his boots on the desk, the senior Mountie took a sip and surmised, "Sam probably stole somebody's fish and then took cover down the shore… before the storm hit. Those Blacks were always up to something…"

"What if the boy is telling the truth, sir?"

With his arm stretched out and his empty cup wavering, he ordered, "Give me another splash of that coffee, and don't swallow shit from a bad source."

"Yes, sir."

Down on the wharf, Junior Black sat over the empty space where the boat with the broken jib used to be. He knew everyone in Slate Harbour wouldn't understand why he would miss a father who had a bad reputation of mistreating him and his mother. For Junior, it didn't matter about the accusations or the insinuations that they smeared upon Sam Black. It was all speculation for a boy who grew up in a shelter of suspicion built upon lies. Born under a cloud of deception, Junior Black didn't know the difference between the weight of a lie and the gravity of the truth. From the wharf, he could see every wave that shattered upon the rocks as he sat and waited for sunrise. He would not leave until the only father that he had ever known came home in the boat with the broken jib.

Chapter 11
Hunt of Hopelessness

Before the sun came up, an assembly of searchers began to prepare a plan that would provide the best possibility for finding Sam Black. Under the direction of the Coast Guard, they discussed areas on the navigational chart where each group would concentrate. Priority of process and primary interest would include the last known location of Sam Black, which was quickly addressed by the Mounties.

"We have reason to believe Sam Black may have been in the location of Wolf Owl Bank and suggest you consider covering this area within your search grid."

The Coast Guard coordinators did not have the Wolf Owl Bank included in their plan. They believed the missing fisherman would be closer to land but couldn't ignore input from the local police. They just simply inquired, "Why do you have reason to believe the missing vessel would be in this location?" The senior Mountie replied, "We had information suggesting his vessel was in that area, and we believe there may have been a fisherman who had seen him. We'll be checking it out later this morning and will keep you posted." The senior Mountie nodded to the junior

Mountie, and they headed toward the Morgan's Pride for further investigation.

On board the Morgan's Pride, Michael was washing the deck clean of debris when Mounties arrived with their familiar smiles and outstretched hands.

"Good morn'n, b'ys."

"Morning, Michael. I see you're not joining the search group today…"

"No… I have engine problems today… What brings you guys aboard?"

"Just checking leads regarding Sam Black."

"And?"

"You were fishing on Wolf Owl Bank yesterday?"

"Yes."

"Was Sam Black there, as well?"

Michael Morgan wasn't a stupid man and knew by the presence of the Mounties and the nature of the question that someone had told them Sam Black was on Wolf Owl Bank. He had known these Mounties well and even played recreational hockey with them on Friday nights at the local arena. He was well-aware that they were police professionals, who picked up on any inkling of a lie. With a sincere nod, Michael Morgan replied, "Yes… When I was leaving, I saw Sam Black off in the distance… On the southern end of Wolf Owl Bank."

"Right… So, you didn't have contact with him, but you saw him?"

"That's correct."

"Well, this is a big help, Michael… We knew you could be counted on…"

"Let's hope they find him…"

"I'm sure they will…"

"Just one thing before you leave…"

"What's that, Michael?"

"Who told you that I knew Sam was on Wolf Owl Bank?"

"I couldn't tell you his name, but I can say this, Michael… The boy is a chip off the old block…"

"Thanks."

"See you up to the arena on Friday night, Mic."

On the police radio, the senior Mountie was quick to call the Coast Guard and confirm the last-seen location of Sam Black. The Mountie was direct in pointing out, "I wouldn't waste time close to the land, I would suggest you concentrate on the southern end of Wolf Owl Bank…"

"Roger that… We'll send all units in that direction at once…"

"Good luck… And keep us posted."

The sea was as smooth as oil as the team of searchers spread out and headed in the direction of Wolf Owl Bank. Up above in the bright blue sky, the rescue helicopter buzzed their heads, heading for the perimeter of the shore. In the event, the boat with the broken jib had washed ashore, they would see it clearly contrasting the black rocks and dark beaches. The local Coast Guard had left with the assumption that all the areas of interest would be thoroughly searched and every anomaly explored, to ensure the best possible outcome.

Whether dead or alive, the option of coming home without a body was a worst-case scenario for the Coast Guard and the victim's family. Unfortunately, it was an all too familiar story that played out time and time again in the small fishing communities that dotted the Newfoundland coastline.

On the southern part of Wolf Owl Bank, with diminished wind and dead calm water, the debris field was not hard to find. It could be seen from the Coast Guard's high bridge, floating as far as the looking-glass could see. Wood portions of the boat tangled with fishing trawl tubs and net marking balloons, told of a tragic end for the departed skipper. The only part that resembled some sort of vessel was the stern that carried a broken jib and a tattered nameplate.

"Coast calling RCMP detachment... Do you have a copy... Over."

"This is the RCMP detachment... Go ahead... Over."

"We have found Sam Black's boat... His nameplate was taken from the debris field."

"What about Sam?"

"Negative... No sign of Sam Black's body..."

"Repeat the last message... Over."

"Sam Black's body has not been found... Over."

"Roger that..."

"We'll collect the debris from the site."

"Roger."

Back at the RCMP station, it was normal to pass the buck when tragic news had to be given. The senior Mountie placed the radio receiver back on the set, looked at his subordinate, and said, "Call the priest Constable... And tell him, he has to make a visit to Lucy Blacks."

"Are they sure he's dead, sir?"

"Well, Constable, they're out on Wolf Owl Bank ten miles out among the remains of Sam Black's boat in bone-chilling waters… There's nothing left of Sam Black after the king-crabs had their way…"

"Will we be doing a further investigation into Sam's death, sir?"

Sitting up straighter than normal, the senior Mountie placed his hands out and exclaimed, "There was a major storm that came and went, leaving nothing but splinters out on Wolf Owl Bank!" He leaned back in the old oak chair and continued his assumption, "Sam Black drowned, and his body was lost at sea…" With his sketchy scenario concluded, the senior Mountie placed his black leather boots on the desk and finished with a condescending question, "What's more to add, Constable?"

Trying to assert himself and add support for his supervisor, the junior Mountie replied, "Well, that troublemaker won't be causing any more disturbances within our jurisdiction, sir."

The senior Mountie peered over the top of his glasses at his subordinate. He was ready to put any junior Mountie in their place at any given time. Relaxing his strained eyes, he replied, "My grandfather from Grand Falls used to say, 'Don't throw water on a dead rat, Constable…'"

Confused by the senior Mountie's rodent response, the wide-eyed young Constable inquired, "Excuse me, sir?"

The senior Mountie took a quick glance out the window at the settling sea and didn't clarify his grandfather's beastly wisdom. Without looking at the junior Mountie, he replied, "When you're finished calling the priest, put on another pot of coffee, Constable."

The bags under Father McCabe's eyes had grown bigger with every tick of the clock that hung on the presbytery wall. Sleep was always scarce for Father McCabe, but in times of tragedy, it was totally absent. He was wide awake and ready for duty when the phone rang, echoing off his stark white walls.

"I see… Yes, I will… Goodbye…"

The call from the RCMP detachment office had been short and right to the deadly point. There was no mistaking the reality that Sam Black was never coming back to Slate Harbour. Father McCabe blessed himself slowly, mumbled a prayer for the dearly departed, and walked out the door with his white collar in hand.

In the small community of Slate Harbour, where houses stood shoulder to shoulder in good and bad times, Father McCabe's white-collared walk had been seen by everyone. House by house, blinds shuttered and curtains moved, keeping pace while the word spread faster than he could walk. By the time he arrived to Lucy Black's house, the door was wide open and the wailing had already begun.

"There, there, my child, Sam is in heaven now… He's up with the angels."

Junior Black was not like his mother, who worshiped the church with all her heart. He had been brought up by a father who didn't believe in the church or the people who sat among the pews. Unlike Lucy, who was front and center in the goings and comings of all church activities, Sam Black was always back at home with his son, far from the rhetoric of their religious rantings. He had been hell-bent on keeping Junior away from the clutches of church, and in the end, succeeded with the assurance of a wide separation between heaven and hell.

Under a thick layer of uncontrolled wailing from his mother, Junior Black's tolerance of listening to a priest had become too much to bear. Like his father, he had no time for scripted statements about going somewhere he knew his father didn't believe.

From the dark corner of the room, Junior's voice sliced the air, "How the fook do you know where my fadder is going?"

"You don't understand, Junior," his mother cried.

"I understand your frustration, my son," the priest interjected.

"You understand shit all," Junior grumbled.

His mother dropped to her knees in agony and cried out, "You don't understand, Son, there's more…" In a state of her immense grief, there was no way Junior could understand the gravity of what she was trying to imply. With suspicions of a different kind building in his mind, the weight of moment moved him to say, "You don't know where fadder is go'n, neither do I, but I'm one hundred percent sure where Michael Morgan is go'n…" He walked past the priest, looked at him with his sky-blue eyes, and finished with clenched teeth, "He's go'n to hell, for murdering my fadder…"

Later that evening, when the sea was calm and Lucy Black regained her composure, Father McCabe called and prompted Lucy to light a candle down at the church. Away from her son's stormy suggestions, it would be a safe harbor where the sanctuary of the church could help settle her waves of grief. Immersed within the smell of the heavy oak pews, Father McCabe took a deep breath when the door opened, and Lucy walked slowly up the aisle.

Lucy Black went straight for the candles, brushing by Father McCabe along the way. The priest stepped up to her side and said, "These sad days will pass, my child…"

"It's like someone punched me in the stomach, Father."

"Where do you go from here, Lucy?"

"I'm not leaving Slate Harbour."

"I'm talking about Junior… Will you finally tell him?"

"In time…"

"There are no excuses now, Lucy."

"How can I tell him now?"

In the sudden silence, they both watched the simplicity of the flickering flame and its complicated dance of light. The shadows from the candles moved randomly back and forth to the beat of a silent drummer in a mesmerizing pattern. For a moment, they both were in the same pew, each knowing the sensitivity of the situation and the erratic reaction of reality. Watching the burning image of conflict upon the wall, Father McCabe asked, "Do you believe what Junior is implying, Lucy?"

"I don't want to believe Michael Morgan would do that to Sam."

"But, do you believe there's some truth to what he's saying, Lucy?"

"He left our house so angry, Father…"

"IF he has something to do with Sam's death, you will have to encourage him to come forth."

From the intensity on Father McCabe's face, Lucy Black's spontaneous reflex made her blurt out, "Do you know something, Father McCabe?"

The priest reached in, and with his bare fingers, he snubbed out Lucy's candle and said, "What I know is between me and God…"

Early the next morning, Michael Morgan got up before sunrise and scurried off toward the Morgan's Pride. On Sunday, whether they were churchgoers or not, it was usual for most folks of Slate Harbour to sleep in late, which made it the perfect scenario to do some silent repairs. With a quick mix of the paint, Michael was up on the forecastle with brush in hand ready to give the damaged stem a thick coat of deep blue. Just as he leaned over the slippery stem, Uncle Price shouted from nowhere, "What are ya do'n, Mic!" Startled, Michael Morgan replied, "Where the fook did you come from?"

"You know me, b'y! I'm up with the seagulls!"

"Ya almost frightened the shit out of me, Uncle Price."

"What are you doing paint'n so in the early in the morn'n?"

"I wanted to get an early start, that's all…"

"Well, your paint won't stay on the plank, with that early morning dew."

"It'll be fine, Uncle Price."

The dripping dew from the fishing stage behind Uncle Price was not hard to see. In the early morning, just as the sun broke the horizon, the dark shadow of the stage gave way to the rising sunlight that shone warmly on the wet spruce clapboard. With every word they spoke and every second that went by, the illumination of a bad blow slowly came into view.

Through a gap between the Church Steeple and Slippery Squid, the sun rays squeezed through and lit up the

Morgan's Pride while they spoke. In full view with rising sun, they could clearly see the damaged stem of the Morgan's Pride.

"That's a mighty large gouge ya have in yer stem, Mic…"

"Nothing that a bit of paint won't cover, Uncle Price."

"Paint can't cover everything, Mic…"

With the rays of the rising sun directly in his eyes, Michael Morgan couldn't see Uncle Price's face, but could hear his footsteps heading out the wharf and away from his arched face. Looking up at the steeple, he dropped his paintbrush into the sea and stood in the shadow of his church. Under the shinning morning sun, Michael Morgan bowed in reflection for a moment and then he headed to a warm place, where shelter from the heat could be easily found.

Father McCabe had always left his door open and his kitchen chair hauled out. He was ready for anyone who needed someone to lean on at any time. Most of the time, he was alone soaking in his own reflective thoughts, but from time to time, someone would walk in and break the sound of his deafening silence.

Michael Morgan opened his screen door and found Father McCabe placing the black kettle on his clean white stove. Without asking, the priest poured out tea and laid it in front of the empty chair and said, "It will warm you up, Mic…"

"I didn't know where to go, Father John…"

"You came to the right place, Mic."

"I don't know what to do."

"Just tell the truth…"

"It will destroy my family."

"Your family is strong and will support you."

"But killing a man…"

"You caused his death, but you didn't kill him."

"What does that mean?"

"It means you could be acquitted in court."

"Nobody will believe that…"

"I do."

"I don't know, Father…"

"Why don't you speak to Lucy Black, Mic?"

"Lucy may understand, but Junior is like his old man."

"More than you'll ever know, Mic…"

"What do you mean by that, Father John?"

"Never mind… Would you like sugar in your tea?"

In spite of his uneasiness to speak with Lucy Black, and regardless of his concern with seeing her angry son, Michael Morgan decided to visit his old girlfriend. To ensure a major battle wouldn't ensue, he watched and waited until Junior was out of the house and far from earshot.

Lucy Black was sorting out her late husband's clothes in the bedroom when she heard familiar footsteps in the house. She walked into the kitchen and said, "If Junior sees you, he'll split ya in half…"

"I saw him leave earlier."

"He thinks you murdered Sam."

"What do you think?"

"I knew you were crazy when you left for Wolf Owl Bank looking for him… But didn't believe you were crazy enough to kill someone."

"No… I didn't kill Sam, but I may have caused his death…"

"Sounds the same to me."

"I tried to save him, just before he went under…"

"You need to speak to the Mounties, Mic."

"He always hated me… Ever since that night we…"

In a room where past memories had never been placed on the table of truth, Michael's forbidden reminder was hard for Lucy to swallow. It had been years ago, but in a flash, the memory returned fresh and bittersweet. With a taste of reality hanging from the pictured wall, Lucy Black returned to her senses without sending Michael mixed messages.

"You better leave before Junior comes home."

She watched Michael Morgan walk down the steps and then looked toward a box containing Sam's clothes. Year after year, day after day, she had seen Sam come and go, with anger for her and animosity for Michael Morgan. It was a never-ending, swinging door of discontent, and she was now free of him and his heavy footsteps. In peaceful reflection, Lucy Black heard the muffled sound of Sam Black's old truck coming up the winding road, and quickly realized her suffering had not been settled. Left in a sea of sorry for the steps she had taken in life, Lucy was beside herself when she saw Junior step out of his father's truck and walk toward their house. Watching his sky-blue eyes pierce the darkness of the fog, she knew her chains of guilt would never be broken.

At eleven o'clock, the brass bell rang loudly over the small fishing village of Slate Harbour. Sunday mass was not to be missed by most, no matter what the circumstances. The majority of the community were churchgoers and knew, by the tolling of the church bell, that it was time to prepare for the cleansing of souls and the forgiveness of sins. However, on that Sunday, with a funeral service scheduled for eleven thirty, the majority of the community would not be attending or forgiving any sins.

It was no secret that Sam Black's friends were few and far between. He appeared to have a talent for antagonizing most men and angering all women, even if they were amicable. Sam was never satisfied until the tables were bottom up, and the fists were flying freely from face to face. Without a doubt, he had made his mark while he lived in Slate Harbour, and nobody forgot it when the end came. The brass bell could have tolled until it fell off the church tower before most would pay respects or attend Sam Black's funeral service.

Inside the church, only greyhaired regulars were in attendance, sitting behind the family of the two Blacks. Outside the church, the priest waited until the precise time to enter and begin the service. On the side of the church, Uncle Price and Tom the bull stood and smoked until the service ended and free sandwiches were offered up by the family. Everything was in place and ready until Michael Black walked up the church steps and said, "Is there room for one more, Father John?"

Father John McCabe didn't mince his words. In full vestments, he leaned in and said, "Until you confess to the Mounties, I can't permit you to enter the Lord's house."

Michael Morgan glanced over at Uncle Price and Tom the bull, who were blowing smoke and looking toward the beach, and said, "I confessed to you down on the wharf..."

"Until you confess to the Mounties and face the judicial system, we cannot receive you here."

"But…"

"Look, Michael, I have a moral obligation to uphold the sanctity of the church, even if that means turning away a friend."

"But I confided in you…"

"Go and do the right thing…"

Father McCabe pulled the door open, and before he left Michael alone with nowhere to go but down, he finished, "And God have mercy on your soul."

Chapter 12
Tide of Truth

Time and tide waited patiently until the Coast Guard collected as much debris as possible from the boat with the broken jib. In a place where the ocean was normally rough, it was unusual for Wolf Owl Bank to be dead calm. Indeed, the smooth seas made a terrible job tolerable for the captain and crew as they recovered the debris and sifted for items of interest. Unfortunately for the crew, the only objects they found were bits and pieces of the boat and random articles of fishing equipment. For the captain, it appeared nothing of any importance was recovered that could shed light on how and why the vessel sunk beneath the waves on that stormy night. Heading back toward Slate Harbour, his conclusion would contain nothing further to add and nothing additional to investigate. For the search crew, Sam Black would become just another small man lost in a big sea.

The main wharf in Slate Harbour was never built to accommodate a large Coast Guard vessel. The only option was to drop off their load and then moor the large vessel out in the bay. Captain Barrett had considered this scenario earlier but opted to unload the debris on the wharf and then immediately set course for the safety of St. John's harbor. In his mind, there was nothing of importance among the items they had collected, and therefore there was no need to stay for clarification. It would be a simple stop and drop, then throttle up for St. John's harbor.

The Mounties were down on the wharf to greet the large Coast Guard boat as it edged its way in and lashed onto the small Government dock. With the lines secured and the engines still idling, they quickly scurried up to the wheelhouse, where the captain was waiting with a full report that provided no further information. Looking down over the deck from the wheelhouse windows, the senior Mountie said, "So, that's it…" The captain moved about the wheelhouse while he answered, "There's not much to see of interest, officers."

"I agree," the senior Mountie added.

Captain Barrett fiddled with his wheel and then got right to the point. "What do you want us to do with it? You know, we can't stay here unless there was something of relevance among that pile of debris."

"Yes, we understand."

"We'll winch it on the wharf for now, and then you guys can decide what to do with it."

The two Mounties leaned toward the large windows facing the deck, and the senior Mountie said, "We'll call young Junior Black. He may want to pick out some stuff of sentiment value. After that, we'll have it trucked to the dump."

"Fair enough."

Anticipating the exact response, Captain Barrett switched on the outside deck speaker and relayed the expected order. Without further delay, the deckhands were ready with winch hook in hand to hoist the load onto the wharf. By the time the Mounties left the wheelhouse and got down to the gangway, the lines were ready to cast off, and the Coast Guard boat was bellowing out white smoke from the engine stacks.

On the wharf, the junior Mountie glanced curiously at the dumped debris and suggested, "Sir, shouldn't we sift through the debris and check for items of interest?" The senior Mountie didn't even glance at the small mound; he just tighten up his cap and said, "It's a waste of our valuable time, Constable."

"But maybe we can…"

The senior Mountie wasn't listening to any more suggestions from his subordinate. He signaled to move on with his hand and began to walk out the wharf, giving one more order, "Call Junior Black when we get back, Constable."

Later that evening, after the call from the Constable, Junior Black scuffed his way out the wharf and began to search through recovered debris. Unlike what the senior Mountie surmised, he wasn't there to collect mementos or sentimental souvenirs. Junior Black was on a specific mission. The Mounties and the Coast Guard Captain may have considered the collection of debris as meaningless dirt, but for young Junior Black, it was more than they would ever know. Inch by inch, piece by piece, he methodically sifted through the scattered pile, as he specifically searched for hard evidence.

Tom the bull sauntered out the wharf and sat on the side, watching the young man scour the scene without saying a word. Uncle Price was not far behind, chewing tobacco and spitting while he walked. They both nodded and sat side by side next to the weight master's winch. Tom the bull lit up a smoke and said, "There's not much left to yer fadder's boat, Junior."

"Who asked for your opinion?"

"Just say'n, that's all…"

Uncle Price hawked his tobacco up and out toward the debris. The splat struck alongside the broken jib, sending Junior storming toward the two men.

"Don't spit on my fadder's grave!"

"I didn't mean any harm… It just looks like junk to me."

The word 'junk' wasn't far off the true reality, and deep down, Junior knew it. He stepped back and turned around to clearly see a pile of dirty debris, tangled with seaweed and green algae. The broken jib was not hard to miss. It was on top of the pile and stood out like an embattled flag of defeat. Defeated, Junior scuffed over and sat down beside the two men and said, "You're right… It's nut'n but a pile of fook'n dirt…"

Uncle Price hawked another large projectile toward the water and said, "Yes, b'y… It's a fook'n mess, but I'll give ya five bucks for that deflated buoy."

Junior never looked up, and with his head hung down, he replied, "If it's there, ya can have it…"

"It's right in front of ya!"

Junior squinted his eyes, scanned the site, and asked, "Is that what yer look'n at?"

"Yep… It's pok'n out from under the jib sail," said Uncle Price.

Junior got up and went over, and with a short hoist of the downed jib, he hauled out the deflated buoy. For the first time in many days, Junior Black smiled as he stared at the filthy, deflated buoy.

Tom the bull exclaimed, "Not bad for five bucks!"

Uncle Price nodded his head and said, "I'll pump it up, and it will be like new."

With a white-knuckled grip on the buoy, Junior growled, "You'll pump up nut'n…"

Noticing the crazy look upon the young man's face, Uncle Price gingerly asked, "Why are ya keep'n it now, Junior?"

Junior Black rubbed the buoy and looked down upon his dirty treasure. "'Cause it's priceless…"

Uncle Price and Tom the bull didn't ask any more questions; they just gave each a wide-eyed stare. They both knew his father was always a bit sideways, but didn't know his son was completely upside down. Without another word spoken, the two men stood up and strolled quietly out the wharf, while Uncle Price whistled a well-known Newfoundland jig.

Left alone and standing with the buoy in his hands, Junior began to rub as hard as he could. Even though Uncle Price and Tom the bull thought he had gone completely mad, he knew something they didn't know. Junior Black knew that his father never used store-bought buoys. Junior knew full well that Sam Black only used discarded plastic anti-freeze containers and not the costly store-bought ones. The anticipation climaxed with a clean, clear view. Looking at the shined, store-bought buoy in his hands, junior knew it was not his father's.

Young Junior Black had seen that buoy many times in the past. He had seen it in the harbor when the boats were docked at close range and had seen it out at sea when they were at long range. It had been engraved in the dark places of his mind by the continual chiseling of his father, who despised the owner of the buoy. The sight of it sent shivers down his back as he held it tightly in his hands and stared at the registration number, 24601. Without a doubt and with one hundred percent confidence, Junior Black knew it belonged to Michael Morgan, the skipper of the Morgan's Pride.

Junior jumped into his father's truck and sent rocks in all directions from the worn-out spinning tires. The feisty commotion and flying projectiles forced Uncle Price and Tom the bull to run for cover behind the closest fishing stage they could find. From the shelter of the stage, Uncle Price exclaimed, "That boy is fook'n nuts!"

Tom the bull was quick to provide support, "He's just like his crazy fadder... A fook'n nut bag..."

"No... That boy is worse..."

"How can he be worse than Sam Black?"

Uncle Price peeped around the stage corner and watched Junior Black burn his soft rubber tires as he hit the hard pavement. He looked back at Tom the bull and with smacking lips, he answered, "'Cause that young bastard caused me to lose me good spit'n chew."

From the RCMP detachment office, it was easy to see someone coming into their gravel parking lot. The junior Mountie was filling the coffee pot with water when Junior Black's truck hauled in, throwing rocks from its tires.

"Sir! It's Junior Black!"

"Good… I was expecting him… Go get that axe and put it under the counter." "Yes, sir."

With a slam of the truck door and a quick pull of the heavy detachment door, Junior stood at the front counter, and before he said a word, the senior Mountie said, "We've been waiting for you, Junior…"

"You're going to charge Michael Morgan?"

"No…"

"You building a case against Michael Morgan?"

"No…"

"Well, what da fook did ya want with me?"

Based on the quick nod from his supervisor, the junior Mountie placed the axe on the counter and said, "We no longer need this for investigation purposes."

They could have struck junior straight through the heart with that axe, knowing they had no intention of following any kind of lead. Normally, he would have gone off like a bomb, but this time, he kept his explosive temper under control. Junior knew he had something they couldn't ignore and with that, he slammed the dirty, deflated buoy on the clean counter.

The senior Mountie picked up one side of the buoy and said, "What's this buoy doing here?"

"It's not just any fook'n buoy…"

"What is it then?"

"It's Michael Morgan's and it was found among the debris from Wolf Owl Bank…" "I see," said the senior Mountie.

Pointing at Michael Morgan's registration number, Junior Black stated, "You better see this…"

"Isn't that something," the Mountie mused.

"Now what do you think, Mr. Smart-Arse Mountie?"

"I think you should give it back to the rightful owner, Michael Morgan..."

Like the deflated buoy that lay upon the counter, Junior Black lost his wind from words he couldn't comprehend. Lost for speech, Junior's head spun from one Mountie to the other, looking for something or someone to snap him out of his slow-motion nightmare. Understanding the dilemma from the sidelines, the junior Mountie tried to soften the blow when he looked at his supervisor and suggested, "Maybe we can speak to Mr. Morgan about it..."

The senior Mountie's face said it all. In one millisecond, his eyes enlarged to the size of pie plates and his face went beet red. Staring at his subordinate, he snarled, "Let me make this perfectly clear to EVERYONE... The coast guard search field entailed the southern section of Wolf Owl Bank where Michael Morgan had been, so the buoy must have come off his gear in the raging storm." Looking for, and receiving a nod of agreement from the junior Mountie, the senior Mountie continued. "Losing fishing gear in that type of weather is perfectly normal."

Getting another nod of understanding from his subordinate, the senior Mountie glanced over at Junior Black's head shaking back and forth in disbelief. He grabbed the file from the counter, closed it, and said, "The case is closed."

Still shaking his head slowly, Junior Black sternly said, "Not for me..."

Before there was any more discussion on the matter, the phone rang and broke the frosty stalemate. After a brief phone call, the junior Mountie said, "We have to go, sir...

There's a drunk man on the government wharf, and it appears he could fall over the edge." The Mounties grabbed their hats, and senior Mountie strongly suggested, "You'll have to leave." Junior Black took his deflated buoy and said, "I'll be back…" The senior Mountie held open the door to signal the time had expired and replied, "I'm sure you will, Junior…"

While the Mounties raced toward the incident unfolding on the wharf, Junior was left alone in the police parking lot. Dejected, he went to place the deflated buoy under the seat of his father's truck, and by fluke, he found a full bottle of Newfoundland screech. In frustration, he flung the disregarded evidence across the parking lot and latched on to his father's rum. With a twist of the bottle top, he took a long swig and realized his lone battle with the Mounties was finally finished.

The Mounties pulled up on the beach to see a man on the slippery wharf wobble back and forth over the water. From the distance, he was just another stranger, but as they got closer, it was clear to see that the wobbling man was their friend Michael Morgan. At shouting distance, the senior Mountie said, "Easy, Michael… You don't want to go for a cold swim this evening…"

Michael Morgan stepped away from the wharf edge and staggered toward the two Mounties. After a long swallow of his beer, he flicked the empty bottle at the stem of the Morgan's Pride and stammered, "I wish… I wish… I had fallen in…"

"You don't mean that, Michael…" the senior Mountie said.

Drunk, Michael Morgan sputtered, "Father McCabe thinks I need to cleanse my soul... Soul." He stumbled toward the wharf edge and added, "Maybe... Maybe, he's right..."

Without further delay, the senior Mountie placed his arm around Michael Morgan and guided him back to the center of the wharf. At the same time, Martha Morgan was slowly coming out the wharf with arms crossed and a worried look upon her face.

Standing in front of her broken husband, she said, "Well... Well, this is a first..." Michael didn't look at his wife directly in the eyes. He looked at the senior Mountie and stammered, "There's always a first for every... everything..."

After a short ride to the Morgan's house, the Mounties placed passed-out Michael Morgan on the couch and then went outside for a chat with Martha.

"That's not normal for Mic," the senior Mountie said.

"Nothing is usual with Mic these days..." replied Martha.

"What do you mean?"

"Nothing has been the same since that storm... Nothing."

"No doubt about it, the wind blew hard that day, Martha."

"More than you'll ever know..."

"Well, the sea has been pretty calm the last few days, Martha..."

"I know, but the storm inside Mic... Is still blow'n."

"Why do you suppose that is, Martha?"

"I really don't want to think about it or talk about it."

To relieve the obvious pressure upon Martha's face, the senior Mountie placed his hat on and said, "Maybe Mic was just blow'n off some steam…"

Martha Morgan glanced over at the calm sea and softly said, "Maybe so…"

On the ride back to the detachment office, the junior Mountie waited at the stop sign and asked, "Straight to the detachment, sir?"

"No, Constable… Let's go to have a real coffee at the Seascape Cafe."

"Sounds like a good plan, sir…"

"And the coffee is on me, Constable…"

"No need for that, sir…"

"I owe it to you."

"Why?"

"I'll tell you at Seascape Café."

Unlike the exotic name, the Seascape Café was just an ordinary fish and chip joint that served regular drip coffee in paper cups. Normally, coffee would be taken off the burner just before noon, and the deep fryers turned on, but at any time the Mounties came in, a fresh pot would be put back on for their important customers.

There was no order required and none expected when they came in and headed for their usual booth overlooking the bay. They removed their hats and slid into opposite sides of a deep booth with a high back. Placing his hands on the table, the senior Mountie began, "First of all, I have to apologize for going into this case with my eyes closed." The junior Mountie didn't speak while his supervisor elaborated, "I didn't take Junior Black's story seriously. I didn't acknowledge the flattened buoy with the fishing registration number in full view. In addition, even though I did understand Michael Morgan was the last to see Sam Black, I dragged my heels throughout this whole horrible ordeal." The junior Mountie tried to support his superior, when he added, "He was your long-time friend too, sir..." The senior Mountie never addressed his biased behavior; he pretended not to hear the comment as he continued, "But! When I saw with my own eyes... A drunken man unraveling due to an internal conflict... And I heard his wife speak about his troubled mind ever since the night of the storm... Well..." The senior Mountie leaned back on the high back of the booth and carefully continued, "I think you were heading in the same direction, Constable."

"Well, sir, earlier, I thought..."

Before the junior Mountie cleared the air with his previous observations, the senior Mountie interrupted, "Yes... Let's forget about things we overlooked in the past and concentrate on the present..."

"I agree fully, sir."

With the senior Mounties' hands outstretched on the table, he exclaimed, "We're going to place this case back on the table, Constable!"

"That's an excellent idea, sir."

"With Junior Black's evidence, Martha's strange statement, and now Michael's bewildering behavior, it is high time... To take a second look."

"Excellent work, sir."

"Thank you, Constable."

"Are we leaving soon to speak with Junior Black, sir?"

"No... We'll talk to Junior in the morning."

"But shouldn't we go see him now, sir."

"What can happen in a few hours? Drink your coffee."

"With great reluctance, the junior Mountie swallowed hard, and said… Nothing."

Chapter 13
Converging Currents

After leaving the detachment parking lot with a bottle of screech between his legs, Junior Black's blood began to boil with anger as he rumbled up the road with his unravelling thoughts. As he drove through the evening and into the night slurping the strong-screech rum, his thoughts had become disturbingly clear. Junior believed he had provided sufficient evidence to charge Michael Morgan but found himself without any support from the Mounties. In his mind, there was no doubt that Michael Morgan had murdered his father and there was nothing going to be done about it. Hitting the crest of the hill at full throttle, Junior Black determined there would be no more long-winded discussions with the Royal Canadian Mounted Police. He decided there and then, he would finish the screech first, and then take matters into his own hands without further hesitation.

Matthew Morgan had been in the fishing stage and away from the upheaval that he felt at home. Since the storm, the fishing stage was a safer harbor from his father's strange behavior and his mother's sea of tears. There, under the dim lights, he could mend some torn nets without thinking or seeing anyone that mattered to him. In his peaceful state of numbness, away from the madness of home, Matthew was unaware that his low lights had caught the attention of a stormy friend.

Without warning, the old stage door gave way to the impact of Junior Black's boot.

Wavering back and forth in doorway, drunken Junior Black roared, "WHERE THE FOOK IS HE?"

"There's nobody here but me…"

In an unhinged state of madness, Junior raised the axe high in the air, and without time for Matthew to move, he came down with all his might. The axe struck the fish gutting table with such force that it sent splinters flying to the four corners of the stage. With the blade stuck deep into the table, Junior slurred, "When I find that prick, I'll CUT 'EM DOWN…"

Directly under the hanging bulb, Matthew Morgan could clearly see the angry determination in his sky-blue eyes. He was out of control, and there was only one way to bring his friend back down to reality.

"If it makes you feel better, Fadder is not well…"

"He'll be dead when I find him…"

With a dialogue started, Michael's plan to talk him down from his dark place would begin.

"Junior, I think this all started a long time ago…"

"Is this more shit from the other night?"

"I tried to tell ya the other night, Fadder told me that he dated your mother."

"What the fook are you say'n, Morgan?"

"Wait! It was only for one night!"

"ARE you say'n, Mudder was a WHORE?"

"No… no… they were split up for a short while, Junior."

His plan to talk a drunken man down didn't seem to have the effect Matthew hoped. Junior placed his hand on the axe which was lodged deep into the table, and said, "You're just as fook'n crazy as your old man…"

"What I'm trying to say is, their hate for each other was based on their love for one woman!"

"That don't justify murder… Morgan."

"It had to be an accident… My Fadder wouldn't kill anybody!"

Junior Black had heard enough lies for the rest of eternity. He had placed the clear evidence on the Mountie's table and found no justice. He told nothing but the truth, and nobody would listen. Now, with these huge lies coming from his former friend, he couldn't take it anymore, and someone was going to pay. Placing his hand on the lodged axe, he released it and grabbed onto Matthew's coat, while staring straight at him. Matthew quickly grabbed onto Junior's coat in return, and the dance of hate began.

As mad and crazy as Junior Black was, he had no intention of fatally hurting his friend.

He intended on giving him two blackened eyes for taking his mother's good reputation in vain.

Then, he would find the murderous Michael Morgan and take justice into his own hands. Out through the large opening, where the fishermen came and went, they scuffed their way to the impending beat. Slowly, inch for hateful inch, they pushed and shoved until they were outside on the landing edge, over the large shore rocks. Then, one man broke their hand free and struck the other with a single hard punch that landed fair and square. A young man teetered for a moment on the slippery round log, then lost his footing and slid over the side of the stage landing. With calm water and no wind blowing, the deadly thud could be easily heard echoing off the rocks that surrounded the seashore.

The dangerous dance had unexpectedly ended, with one quick note of hate and a never-ending chorus of regret. Back into the stage and out the door, as fast as he could run, there was only one place for him to go. He quickly reached the side of his best friend to lift his head from the rock and hear his final words, "Revenge is not worth it, my friend…" From his own sky-blue eyes, he could not believe that he had seen his best friend Matthew Morgan die in his bloodied arms. In a drunken panic, he scrambled over the rocks beneath the stage and away from his dead friend. Reaching his truck, he found the last drop of screech and swallowed it down to ease the pain. Too drunk to walk, Junior Black drove his truck home where he finally passed out in the secluded driveway.

The next morning, the tide came in on the rocks and on the body of young Matthew Morgan. It was early, but as usual, Uncle Price did his usual stroll out the wharf while he had his normal chew of tobacco. By the weigh-master's shed, Uncle Price spit his chewing tobacco straight out toward Morgan's stage and noticed gulls landing close to an old log. It had appeared to Uncle Price that the log drifted onto the rocks with the incoming tide. Watching the log closely, he noticed it didn't move naturally with the rise and fall of the ocean.

Uncle Price stood to his feet as Tom the bull began to step onto the government wharf.

Before Tom the bull got any further, Uncle Price pointed, and shouted, "What's that over by Michael Morgan's stage?"

"Hold on, I'll check…"

Tom the bull was as big as a moose and clumsy as a bag of hooks. Carefully, he wobbled his way over the slippery rocks until he got to the place where Uncle Price was pointing. As he looked closer, a large sea swell came in and turned the unknown entity toward the big clumsy man. In the cold morning tide, Tom the bull came face to face with the corpse of young Matthew Morgan. The strange shriek that came from the shocked man made every hair on Uncle Price's back stand on edge. From the rocks of the seashore, Tom the bull shouted at the top of his lungs:

"GO GET THE FOOK'N MOUNTIES!"

In minutes, the Mounties were on the rocks placing yellow caution tape around the stage and surrounding area. After measuring the height of the fall and seeing the rocky area below the stage landing, the senior Mountie determined that Matthew Morgan died of an accidental death.

He was in the fishing stage above the accident scene and about to close the case until the junior Mountie walked in and joined him.

"Is the scene secured down below, Constable?"

"Yes, sir, but Michael Morgan is here, and extremely distraught."

"Then we'll wrap this up here and I'll join Michael Morgan down below."

"Wrap it up, sir?"

"But sir, we haven't searched the stage."

"The things you'll find in this stage, you'll see in all stages; there's nothing to search."

Performing a quick glance around the stage, where knives, prongs, and other items were sticking out from every corner, the junior Mountie suggested, "Shouldn't we consider that axe, sir?"

Pointing in two different places around the stage, the senior Mountie pointed at one short axe and another long axe and said, "There are three axes in total, and that's normal to see in a fishing stage, Constable. In addition, there are no cuts or stab wounds on the body. The young man simply slipped on the edge of the stage landing and fell to the rocks below."

"But the axe that's stuck into the fishing gut table is different, sir…"

"Why is that, Constable?"

Pointing toward the axe that was deeply lodged into the gutting table, the junior Mountie said, "That's the axe Junior Black brought into the detachment office, and that's the one we gave him back yesterday."

The senior Mountie closed his book and commanded, "Let's go pick him up for questioning!"

In a small community, it wasn't necessary for Mounties to deliver bad news. Sometimes words would spread faster than they were spoken, and in this case, the Morgan's grief was well underway.

On the wet rocks under the stage landing, Michael Morgan was in complete shock. The senior Mountie approached him and said, "I'm sorry for your loss, Mic…"

"But… How could he fall from a place that he knew so well?"

"Don't worry, Mic, we're looking into it…"

"What do you mean, you're looking into it?"

"Never mind, Mic, we have it under control…"

"What do you have under control?"

"We have to go… There's work to do."

"Where are you headed?"

"We'll be back… We need to question you again, about Sam's death."

Watching the body of his son lifted from the rocks beneath their stage wasn't something Michael Morgan was prepared for. His grief went beyond the parameters of sanity and sent him back to a dark deep place in his mind. Shaking his head, Michael quickly considered the Mountie's vague response about looking into something and came to a quick conclusion. He swiftly busted through the yellow caution tape and entered his fishing stage to find out what they were looking into.

Under the radiant morning rays that shone through the dirty stage window, it only took Michael Morgan one quick glance. From the doorway, he saw his familiar gutting table and couldn't miss the glare that reflected off an unfamiliar axe. The foreign blade had busted through the two-inch plank, and a peculiar handle was sticking out, perpendicular to the table. As he moved closer to the axe and clearly saw the homemade handle, Michael Morgan knew exactly what the Mounties were looking into. Now, it would be a race to finish, to find the young man who murdered his son in cold blood and left the familiar black mark in full view.

After waking up in the cab of his truck by the side of their house, Junior came to his senses and rushed inside to find his mother Lucy following his every footstep. As Junior rustled around the house preparing a backpack, the tension was building minute by minute. From room to room, he slammed drawers and banged doors while opening and closing them, searching for random things to take with him. Watching her son scrambling about in a mad panic, his mother knew it was time to tell the truth before her son would do something that they both would regret.

While following from room to room, she said, "We need to talk…"

"Did you see my brown coat?"

"There's something I need to tell you…"

"Have you seen the sleeping bag?"

"It's really important…"

"I'll need some canned food for up on the hill…"

In the pantry, at her wits end, Lucy Black stood and shouted at the top of her lungs:

"LISTEN TO ME!"

Junior stopped moving about and looked at his distraught mother, while she wiped her face and began to speak. "Sam wasn't your real father…"

"What are you say'n, Mudder?"

"I'm try'n to tell you that your real father is Michael Morgan…"

In a split second, the words that she had whispered to Father McCabe in the confessional box were finally released, and her job was done. She collapsed in grief upon the cold tiles while her son dropped his backpack in shock.

"Noooooo… That's not true…"

With no response from the sobbing woman, Junior Black stumbled out the door, heading toward his truck. In a trance-like state, he robotically placed the truck in gear and headed for a higher place to consider his mother's wild revelation.

Minutes later, Lucy Black's front door swung open and someone stepped in. Lucy cried out, "Junior, is that you?"

"No… It's me…"

Michael Morgan stood and watched the shattered Lucy upon the kitchen tiles. He went to her side and demanded, "Where's Junior?"

Sobbing uncontrollably, she replied, "I don't know… Maybe up on the hill…"

"When I find him, I'll kill that young bastard!"

"You don't understand, Mic…"

"I understand that he murdered my son…"

The deadly accusation brought Lucy quickly to her feet and snapped her out of her personal grief. She wiped her eyes, "What do you mean?"

"Matthew has been killed, by the hands of Junior…"

"That can't be…"

"Now it's his time to pay…"

"You can't hurt him, Michael!"

"Why can't I get revenge?"

Collapsing, she said, "Because Junior is your son…"

Michael Morgan went into shock and couldn't fathom Lucy Black's deepest secret. He was completely traumatized over losing a son he loved and gaining a son he hated. In his state of confusion, the only thing he could do was to keep going and find the killer of his beloved son.

The Mounties may have been going around in circles to find Junior Black, but Michael Morgan had a good notion where he could be found. Looking up toward the hilltop, on a straight line of sight from Lucy's house, Michael was pretty sure Junior was watching them from up above. Many times, when Junior and Matthew were young kids, they would hike up the hill that overlooked Slate Harbour. It was a place they could get away from a family feud that had been going on forever. Michael Morgan knew that even though he and Sam had always been fighting enemies, Matthew and Junior had always been good friends. With his foot to the floor, he headed upward, hoping to find Junior where shelter was found so many years ago.

Distraught Lucy Black gathered herself together and called the only other person who knew her deepest secret. Father McCabe picked up the phone and was given a quick synopsis that entailed a story of revenge and retaliation. With no time to spare, he splashed holy water over his head and sped off to pick up Lucy along the way.

On the edge of Slate Harbour, the two Mounties had stopped on the side of the road to finish cold coffee and consider their next step. In a place where the road veered left and right, they were sipping coffee and studying possible search scenarios when Father McCabe and Lucy passed them in a cloud of dust and headed left. Normally, everyone veered right, where the dirt road connected to the paved road. It was very unusual to see someone veer left, unless there was something of interest high upon the hill.

Wiping the dust from his eyes, the senior Mountie started the patrol car and said to the junior Mountie, "Buckle up, we're going to follow that car."

"Seems like we're always just behind the priest, sir."

"What do you mean, Constable?"

"Death or family disturbance, Father McCabe seems to always be first, and we seem to always be last to pick up the pieces..."

"In this case, you may be right, Constable... I can smell a family disturbance that reeks of death..."

Chapter 14
Rendezvous of Revenge

High on the hill overlooking Slate Harbour, Junior Black was at the lowest point in his young life. In trying to comprehend that his father had been murdered by a fellow fisherman and his best friend died by his own hands, Junior Black believed he couldn't go any lower. That is, until he saw Michael Morgan crest the hill and put him in the sights of his rusty grill.

There was no time to run and nowhere to go, with the only way down blocked by Michael Morgan's truck. Slowly, Michael Morgan got out of his truck and walked toward Junior with a scowl smeared on his face and a shot gun shaking in his hands. From a short distance, with the midday sun high up above, Michael Morgan could feel the heat from Junior's sky-blue eyes burning a hole right through his damaged soul. As he walked slowly toward his newfound son, the questions began.

"How could you kill my son, so coldly?"

"How could you murder my fadder, in cold blood?"

The unanswered questions hung in the air, like the cold fog that hovered over the harbor down below, until Michael Morgan confessed, "I did strike his boat… But as God as my witness, Junior... He was alive, and I tried to reach out... He wouldn't accept my help, and in the end, he cut his own rope that sent him to the bottom..."

"That sounds like something the old man would do... He hated the ground you walked on... He always had suspected you and Mudder..." Looking over the cliff, Junior continued, "Now I know why he'd never accept your help... His suspicions were true."

Michael Morgan nodded and said, "Your mother and I only had one night, a night when we both thought Sam had left her for good..." Watching the young man squirming where he stood, Michael Morgan tried to explain, "You knew his temper! On that day, he hit your mother, she swore she'd never see him again..." After a short uncomfortable silence, Michael Morgan went on, "I never did like the guy back then, but I did have feelings for your mother... She knew I did too, and she reached out for someone to lean on... We were young... And the rest was history, with you as my son..." Standing with the shotgun lowered by his side, he sincerely said, "I never knew you were my son..." Again, silence from both men, until Michael Morgan continued, "But suspicion must have grown inside of Sam, and with every year his anger toward me grew... I was always defending myself with him and never understood why he hated me so much. His hate pushed me to hate back, to the point I lost who I really was... On the day we were out on Wolf Owl Bank, there was a point where I wanted to turn away, but when I saw him spewing hate toward me again, I lost it for a moment and struck his boat... I didn't mean to cause his death, but I did, and I'm sorry... For that senseless revenge, I'll be sorry for the rest of my life..."

The snarly face of young Junior Black began to soften, and his frosty demeanor began to melt as he spoke, "I accused you of murdering Fadder, but Matthew tried to tell me different... He told me of your fling with Mudder, but I don't think he knew the depth of that fling... At that moment, with my Mudder's honor being questioned by the son of a murderer, I lost it and was pushed over the edge of sanity... I forced him to fight... I struck him hard... He slipped on the slippery stage landing and fell to the rocks below... I didn't mean to kill him... I only wanted to hurt him..." Junior's eyes filled to capacity as he sucked in his emotions and said, "Matthew Morgan was the best friend I ever had..."

Standing with the shotgun in his hands, Michael Morgan could see the river of tears roll down his sky-blue eyes. He swallowed hard and said, "It seems we were both caught in circle of hate and revenge..."

The shaking son stared his father in the eyes and said, "Go ahead, shoot me, Fadder... I deserve it for killing my best friend..."

Junior's sincere death plea hit Michael Morgan right between his sky-blue eyes. He could clearly see the pain plastered on his son's face that had been caused by the senseless cycle of retribution. Michael knew the violence had carved a permanent scar on their souls. At that moment, he realized retaliation had done too much damage. He decided there and then, the flame of revenge would be finally quenched.

"Junior, I don't know how we'll move forward from here as father and son, but I do know that this cycle of revenge will end here today..."

Through a cloud of dirt and dust, Father McCabe and Lucy Black arrived to find Michael Morgan holding Junior at gunpoint. Father McCabe walked slowly toward the two men, and Lucy Black rushed toward her husband's truck. Before any words of forgiveness from the priest could be spoken, Lucy removed the shotgun from her late husband's truck.

Unbeknownst to Junior, Sam Black's shotgun had been behind the seat the whole time. Like Michael Morgan, his father always carried the shotgun in case he needed to take down unexpected wild game. Lucy had been with Sam on many occasions when the gun was brought into hunting action. With continual practice, she had become a better shot than her husband Sam.

Now, with her son's life threatened by her old lover, she latched onto the gun. She believed that if there was a spark remaining in Michael Morgan's flame of revenge, it would be quenched with a gun that was locked and loaded.

Michael Morgan had no intention of killing Junior or anyone else on that morning. In a seemingly slow-motion move, he lifted up the gun with the good intention of throwing it over the cliff and found himself sending a wrong message. From a fair distance, Lucy Black had received a mixed message and sent a clear response. She squeezed the trigger and sent a hard slug into the soft breast of Michael Morgan.

The sound from the unexpected shotgun blast shook the still morning air and sent shock waves in all directions. The sound waves vibrated through the startled priest who had no warning of where the shot came from and why it had been fired. The waves pierced the heart of a son who had finally heard the sound of forgiveness from the lips of a fallen father. The shock waves finally gave way to the distant sound of Michael Morgan's rifle echoing off the cliffs as it bounced its way down toward the base of the hill.

Lucy Black walked slowly toward Father McCabe with the smoking gun still aimed at the body of Michael Morgan. He softly laid his hands on the barrel and gently removed it from her hands without resistance. She looked at the priest and sobbed, "I couldn't let him kill my son, Father McCabe…"

Even though Sam Black's rifle was designed to fire twelve-gauge bullets, it had been loaded with a single slug. That one lump of solid lead could take down a bull moose with one shot at a long range from the right shooter. From a distance, she was very aware that her keen sights had been aimed at the center of Michael Morgan's chest. Lucy didn't have to look because she knew that her shot had been deadly accurate.

Michael Morgan was fading fast when the Mounties crested the hill and headed for the scene. He didn't know that Lucy had fired the gun, as she, Junior, and Father McCabe surrounded his dying body. Michael smiled at Lucy, coughed, and said, "Is that you, Lucy?"

In a river of tears, Lucy replied, "I'm so sorry, Michael…"

With the Mounties joining the crowd, Michael Morgan had no idea where the bullet came from or who shot the gun. Fading in and out, he could only see Lucy's face glowing under the shinning sun. "Tell Junior…"

"I'm here, Michael."

"Junior?"

"Yes, I'm here… You'll be alright; the Mounties will take you to the hospital…"

"No, Junior… The only place I'm going is with Matthew…"

Lucy squeezed Michael's hand and said, "Matthew is with God…"

"No, Lucy… I can see Matthew in front of me."

With a gasp, he asked, "Junior?"

"Yes…"

"Don't, don't… be like your father… revenge is not worth it."

"But you're my father now…"

"Revenge is not… not worth it, Son…"

Gasping in quick convulsions, Michael Morgan searched the shadows that surrounded him and found Lucy right by his side. With his last suck of salt air, he looked at her with his sky-blue eyes and said, "I… I guess… Sam always knew, I… I, never stopped loving you…"

Father McCabe bent down, closed his sky-blue eyes, and recited the last rights over the deceased Michael Morgan. This triggered the senior Mountie to begin a line of questioning aimed at Junior Black.

Standing over the dead body, the senior Mountie looked at Junior and asked, "Who shot him?" Before his mother could reply, Junior went to the defense of his mother, "He was going to fire at me, but I shot him first."

"Are you saying he tried to kill you because you knew he killed your father?"

"Yes… He knew I wouldn't stop until he was behind bars."

"That makes sense…"

"Where are the guns?"

"My gun is there, in front of my truck."

The senior officer glanced over at the junior constable and said, "Process that for evidence."

"Yes, sir."

He returned his attention to Junior and asked, "Where's Michael's gun?"

Junior pointed toward the edge of the cliff and said, "It flung out of his hands and over the edge."

The senior officer glanced over at the junior constable and said, "Check to see if the gun is there, Constable."

"I can see the gun shinning at the bottom, sir."

"Fetch it and bag it for evidence, Constable."

"Yes, sir."

As it happened, the Mounties had already redirected their focus on the death of Sam Black. They had reconsidered the case, based on the evidence Junior had placed on the table and the guilty behavior exhibited by Michael Morgan. Their intention was to find Junior and question him about the death of Matthew Morgan and then charge Michael Morgan for the death of Sam Black. In light of the events that unfolded up on the hill over Slate Harbour, it appeared things were finally making sense. If Junior's story could be corroborated by a certain person's input, the case would be concluded.

The senior Mountie continued with a setup for the final answer. "Are you saying, Junior, that Michael thought YOU killed Matthew… in retaliation for HIM murdering Sam?"

Junior looked at the priest standing by his side and replied, "Yes, that's exactly right, Constable."

"So, it was in self-defense?"

"Yes..."

The senior Mountie tilted his head down and peered at the priest, over his black-rimmed glasses. Looking directly into his eyes, he asked, "Is this true, Father McCabe?"

Father McCabe had been tested before and found his silence had done more damage than good. In light of the events, he knew that the secret in the confessional box should have been shared. He also knew that the secret Michael spilled under the broken light pole should have been spoken. Looking at the wake of death and revenge that had produced, he understood the implication of his silence and the ramifications that had resulted. Father McCabe was a good priest who had followed the letter of the cardinal law with dedication and devotion, but on that day, with the eyes of the law and the broken life of young Junior Black hanging in the balance high above Slate Harbour, Father McCabe answered with an ambiguous lie.

"It's the truth, as I know it..."

The junior Mountie appeared from the edge of the cliff with sweat on his brow and the Michael Morgan's rifle in his hands.

The senior Mountie closed his notepad and said, "Well, that settles that... With the undisputable word from the priest and the concrete evidence from the dead hand of Michael Morgan, we can close this case with confidence." Then he looked at Junior and continued, "But we still have the case of Matthew Morgan unless you can share what you know."

Junior didn't face the Mountie. He looked toward Father McCabe and said, "Father McCabe, as God as my witness... My best friend Matthew slipped on the wet landing and fell.

It was an accident. I would never have killed my best friend… Never.”

The senior Mountie turned to his subordinate and said, “Call the coroner, and let's put all this behind us.”

“What should I write in, as the cause of death, sir?”

“In the case of Michael Morgan, it was self-defense.”

“And in the case of Matthew Morgan, sir?”

“It was accidental, Constable. Just an unfortunate accident.”

“And, what about Sam Black… For the record, sir?”

“In the case of Sam Black, it was pure revenge, Constable.”

From high on top of Slate Harbour hill, the cold wind picked up and sent the fine sand swirling around the dead body of Michael Morgan. In a place where lovers swept in under the full moon and secret stories were spilled in the light of the day, the landscape would be forever changed. On the sharp ledges of that shale cliff, retribution had gained a foothold in the lives of two families and chiseled out a vengeful mark. While they surrounded the body of Michael Morgan, a draft of cold wind blew in from the distant sea, prompting the priest to rub his hands and say, “That northerly wind goes right through a man's soul.” The senior Mountie closed his notepad, while suggesting to the priest, “That wind is coming from the east, Father.” With his head hung down, Junior shook his head and corrected the senior Mountie, “Nooooo… It's blow'n in from the east by southeast.” The Mountie wasn't accustomed to being corrected. He leaned toward the young man and sarcastically replied, “Seems like Sam taught you the points of the compass along with showing you how to shoot a gun." For a moment, they stood in silence, while a gust of wind sent loose sand slicing by their sides. When the wind subsided, Lucy Black said, "Well Mr. Mountie… Sam taught me about navigation and how to shoot a gun, but that doesn't have anything to do with the direction of that wind." The Priest looked down at the corpse and stuttered, "It… It's an ill breeze that blows over the body of Michael Morgan." Lucy Black slowly turned her face into the wind. She looked in the direction of Wolf Owl Bank and finished, "Today, that cold wind is come'n from the darkest part of the compass."

www.ingramcontent.com/pod-product-compliance
Lightning Source LLC
Chambersburg PA
CBHW070802160726
48004CB00001B/292